The Pastor's Admin

HIS SECRETS OR MY SANITY!

Dedication

This book, like all the rest, is dedicated to those of you who continue to believe in and support, book after book!

Please don't stop. Your support and encouragement is the fuel I, we, need to keep writing!

Lakisha's Gratitude

As always, to God whom I owe everything. If it wasn't for the gift He so graciously gave, I wouldn't be able to do what I love.

To my husband, Willie, my children Gabrielle and Christopher; thank you for sharing a piece of me with the world. To those family members, who support everything I do, THANK YOU!

And to every one of you, who support Lakisha, THANK YOU! I would not be the author I am without readers like you. It is because of you purchasing, reading, reviewing and recommending that pushes me to be greater with each release. Thank you from the bottom of my heart!

LaQuisha's Gratitude

For this I take nothing...All to Him (My God) I owe!

To you my family, my loves, my friends and my supporters I thank you from the bottom of my heart for believing in this gift that God has bestowed upon me and Lakisha to do (her more so than me; I am just along for the ride).

Your support in this journey has been amazing and unwavering from the very beginning and I pray that with each word we type, each prayer that you read, each tear that you shed and each laugh that you give that you feel our hearts because we leave them on each page.

Keep reading and believing because Twins Write 2!

The Pastor's Admin

HIS SECRETS OR MY SANITY!

Prologue

Sound of my phone vibrating

"Ah shit," I say feeling around for my phone, finally touching it on the nightstand.

"Hello." I answer barely opening my eyes.

Nobody says anything.

"Hell-lo!" I say blinking a few times to see the caller id clearer.

"Joe?" I blow into the phone.

Sounds of shuffling.

"Aw," someone moans.

What in the entire hell? "Joe?"

"Ooh God!" A woman's voice says.

I know this bastard did not butt dial me while having sex. I call his name again. When I hear what sounds like the phone dropping, I sit up in the bed.

"JOE!"

Still nothing so I release the call before dialing his number back.

No answer.

Shaking my head.

I put the phone back on the nightstand before grabbing the cup sitting there and swallowing all the water in it.

I look around the room, thankful to at least be at home because I cannot for the life of me remember what in the hell happened. I see scarves laying on the bed and a wine bottle on the floor but wine has never left me feeling like this.

I swing my legs over the edge of the bed and stand up but when my feet touch the floor, I stagger.

I close my eyes and hold my head to stop the swirling. "Oh God."

I barely make it to the toilet, before emptying my stomach contents.

I sit there a minute trying to get myself stable enough to stand up. Finally pulling up to the sink, I turn on the water, hoping the coldness will sober me up.

It doesn't.

I rinse my mouth and look at my reflection trying to remember something, anything about the night.

I sigh.

Walking back to the bedroom, my foot kicks the wine bottle. I bend down to pick it up when my eyes focus in on my purse that's open on the floor.

I sit the bottle on the dresser and reach for my purse only to see keys laying on top of it. I raise them up and realize the second key chain that hold keys for Joe's house, the church and my desk are gone.

I rush over to grab my phone, dialing Joe's number.

"Answer! Come on Joe!"

No answer.

I try again. "Damn it! Come on Joe, answer the freaking phone."

When he still doesn't answer, I send a text.

"Joe, please call me. I think you're in trouble."

I lay the phone down and grab the cup from the nightstand to get more water. After walking out the bathroom, I pick up my phone to see Joe still hasn't responded, so I call him again.

No answer.

"Lord, please let this man be okay." I mumble while walking in circles.

After a few minutes, my phone vibrates with a text.

JOE: Dee, I need your help.

ME: Haven't you see my calls? Why won't you answer the phone?

JOE: I cannot talk. I just need you to come.

ME: Come where?

JOE: My house.

ME: Is it Torre?

JOE: No, just come, please!

ME: I'm on the way but you better not have another woman in that house!

I stop when it feels like I'll be sick again but taking a few deep breathes help. Walking over to the dresser to grab some underwear, I see the wine bottle, again and then it hits me, this bitch drugged me.

I quickly slip on some panties and a bra before putting on a pair of pajama pants, a sweatshirt and UGG Boots.

Grabbing my purse, I get to the car and push the start button. My hand grabs the gear shift to put the car in reverse but I stop because something doesn't feel right. I try to call Joe again but he doesn't answer so I make another call.

"911, what's your emergency?"

"Uh yes, I think my boss is in trouble."

"In trouble how ma'am?" The dispatcher asks.

"I don't know but can you please send somebody just to check?"

"I can but it'll be a minute before I can get a car there unless there is something else going on?"

"I can't explain it ma'am but he sent a text asking me to come to his house but now he won't answer my calls. I really believe he is in danger."

"What's the address ma'am?"

"1001 Fen Bark Hollow in Cordova."

"The name of the person you believe to be in trouble?"

"Joseph Thornton."

"And your name?"

"Daphne Gary."

"We will have a car sent."

"Please hurry."

I hang up and send a text.

"Joe, something doesn't feel right so I am sending the police."

Twenty minutes later, I hurriedly pull in front of Joe's house and get out. There is a police car in the driveway so I rush to the door. When I get there, the door is pushed opened and I see an officer standing inside.

"What's going on?"

"Ma'am, you can't go any further." He says stopping me in the living room.

I look around but I don't see Joe and the only other light on is in the master bedroom.

"This is my boss' house. I am the one who called for the welfare check so can you please tell me what's going on?"

"Ma'am, you will need to wait outside."

"Joe!" I scream. "Joe! Please just tell me what is happening."

"I cannot give you any information. If you wait outside, a detective will be here to speak to you."

I turn, acting like I'm headed outside but instead I push pass him running towards the master bedroom. Getting to the door, my heart drops into my stomach at the scene.

"Oh my God, no!" I cry as the officer pulls me out the room and into the living room.

"You will need to stay here." He says as the sounds of sirens fill the streets.

"Are they – are they dead?" I ask through tears as EMTs run in.

"Ma'am, please just stay here."

A few minutes later, they walk out shaking their head at the officer as he gets on his radio. "Dispatch, we have a 10–70 at my location. Roll a homicide detective and crime scene."

Daphne

10 years ago

I walk through the double doors of the church with a printed copy of the ad in my hand. I stop at the front desk but no one is there. I look at my watch, hoping I didn't miss the person hiring because I really need this job.

I wait a few seconds and decide to find the Administrative Offices myself. I turn at the end of the hall but no one is sitting at that desk either. I was about to leave when I see the Pastor's door slightly open.

I knock.

"Hello, is anyone there? I am here about the ad. Hello."

No one answers so I push the door open and go in.

Walking around the corner, "Oh my God!" I drop my bag and the paper I am holding when I encounter a man coming out of the bathroom with a towel wrapped around his waist.

When he looks up, I start backing up to leave.

"Wait," he says.

"I, um, I am so sorry. I didn't mean to, I um, knocked but no one answered." I say bending down to grab what I dropped.

He smiles. "That's quite alright. What can I do for you?"

"Uh, I was inquiring about the ad but I'll wait outside until you're dressed."

"You don't have too."

"Joe, what is going on here?" A lady asks as soon as I turn to leave.

"Torre, baby, it's not what you think." He stammers.

"I apologize." I say stepping back from her. "My name is Daphne Gary and I'm here about the ad, from National Baptist's Website, for an Administrative Assistant. The door was open, I came in but I had no idea he was in the shower."

She stands there looking back and forth from me to him.

"Ms. Gary, can you please wait outside?" She asks.

"Sure." I say hurrying to leave.

Before I can get the door closed, I hear her beginning to yell.

After a few minutes, the door swings open and she comes storming out. I turn to face her.

"Ma'am, I am so sorry--"

She cuts me off. "I'll be the one conducting your interview. Follow me."

Present Day

"Daphne? Hello." Pastor Thornton says snapping his fingers in front of my face.

"Huh?"

"What has you zoned out?"

"Nothing, why are you here on a Saturday? What do you need?"

"I have a meeting but I'll be back in an hour. You know what? You better make that two."

"And?"

"What has you in this foul mood?"

"Nothing Joe. You have a meeting, I got it."

"You need to get laid." He says.

"You get enough for the both of us."

"You do have a point." He says before walking out, whistling.

I shake my head as I watch him leave, cursing the day I took this job. Hell, a few times I've considered it to be one of the worst mistakes of my life.

Anyway.

Hey, my name is Daphne Gary and I am 38 years old. I've been in the field of administrative work for almost 20 years. I started working at 17, in the office where my mom was a paralegal. I did admin work for one of the firm's partners, twenty hours a week, while in high school.

I enjoyed it because for the most part, this line of work was easy and sometimes rewarding, until Joseph Thornton; correction, Pastor Joseph Thornton.

I've been with him for ten years and three churches. Don't get me wrong, Joe is definitely one of God's chosen who can do what the younger folk say, slay you in the spirit. However, he has demons. BIG DEMONS.

He is handsome and he knows it. He has women throwing themselves at him and let's just say, his flesh is willing and his spirit weak. Yes, I know it should be the other way around but you'll understand what I mean.

Yeah, this Negro is married and has been for ten years to his wife, Torre. They were married a few months before she hired me as the pastor's admin.

Torre is one of those pastor's wives who is easy to love. She is smart, sassy, a nice dresser, funny and very involved in the church. Lately though, the fire she used to have has dwindled and I know the person holding the extinguisher.

I asked her, the other day, why she stays with Joe and you know what she did? She asked me the same question. Funny thing is, I'm just like her; unsure of why I'm still here.

This man has caused me to get grey hairs in places a lady should never be grey. He is what you call, a man whore because he can't ever seem to keep his hands or his penis to himself.

I told him the other day, his penis is like community property and this Negro had the nerve to laugh saying, "Dee, you're crazy."

Whatever!

And just when I think I've seen or heard it all, he manages to come up with a new way to leave me speechless.

I thought things would be better once he started Assembly of God Christian Center, four years ago but being the founder of this church took him to an entirely different level and I don't mean in a good way.

Before you starting wondering, HELL NO, I've never slept with him. Oh he tried, in the beginning but his little thingy has too many miles for me to even entertain. Plus I love the very thing that keeps getting him in trouble. (If you know what I mean.)

Anyway. I can't truthfully answer why I stay but I can tell you one thing. I will not be able to deal with him much longer because it's either going to be his secrets or my sanity.

While I figure it out, here's my story of being the Pastor's Admin.

Joseph

I walk into the conference room with all eyes on me.

"Good afternoon Pastor."

"Gentleman."

"If you could take a seat."

"Deacon Thorpe, why the sudden need for this meeting, especially on a Saturday?"

"Pastor, we will get to that but first, Harper, can you lead us in prayer?" Deacon Thorpe says looking at me.

"Bow your head." Harper says placing his hands together before him.

"Father God, we come to you this evening thanking you for your many blessings. God, we thank you for allowing us to make it here to another meeting. We ask, oh God, that you will guide our thoughts and our words. God, let us be humble servants on today and that everything we do be pleasing in your sight. Don't allow us to get caught up in emotions and carried away with our tongue but let us govern ourselves as the men you've ordained us to be. I pray this prayer in your darling son Jesus name. Amen."

"Amen," we all say together.

"Now, what is this about?" I ask again.

"This meeting is now called to order." Deacon Thorpe's voice roars over the silence in the room. "This is an emergency meeting called in regards to some disturbing news we've received regarding you, Pastor Thornton."

"What kind of disturbing news?" I ask.

"Well, we received a report of misconduct on your part."

I laugh. "Misconduct on my part? By who and what is this claim?"

"The name of the accuser is not important. I can share with you that there is a young lady who is claiming to be pregnant with your child and she is threatening to make it known to the church."

"What does she want?" I ask.

"She is demanding $20,000, a condo in her name and a new car."

I laugh.

"Do you think this is a joke?" Thorpe asks.

"I do but I also find this crazy. There is no way I or this church will meet those demands. Tell her she can do what she wants."

"Wait, just hold on a minute." Deacon Harper says. "We cannot risk the backlash this kind of scandal can cause the church, pastor. We have the mayor coming on Sunday to speak to the congregation, a very generous donation from the Slater family as well as the reputation of this church to uphold?"

"A church I built!"

"We are all aware of that but--" Thorpe says before I cut him off.

"Then you should know that I will not allow some liar to use me for her come up. Let me ask you a question gentleman."

"Go ahead."

"If this woman was indeed pregnant by me, why isn't she wanting me to be a part of the baby's life? All she is asking for is material things. Does anybody else find that odd?"

"We are not in the business to handle your personal affairs, pastor, however we do have a responsibility to this church."

"As do I and if you think I am falling for this trick's game, think again. If I am not willing to give my wife a baby, what makes you think I'll knock up some skank? So, you tell her to do what she

thinks is best but those demands will not be met."
I stand to leave.

"Pastor Thornton, we need to resolve this."
Harper says.

"I've already told you how to resolve it and it's my final answer. Now, if there isn't anything else, I have somewhere to be."

"Fine but don't say we didn't warn you." Thorpe says sitting back in his chair.

"I don't need you warning me about anything. I know every damn thing that goes on in this church and if you think I am surprised by this, you're just as crazy as the one who filed this complaint. She isn't the first to try this foolishness and she won't be the last. As for you, if you want to keep your position, I suggest you remember who's in control here."

Daphne

Joe comes rushing pass me in a huff.

"I thought you said two hours."

He doesn't respond before slamming the door to his office.

An hour later, the intercom sounds.

"Dee, can you come in my office for a minute?"

I hang up without even acknowledging him.

"Dee, did you hear me?"

I open his door. "What can I do for you Pastor?"

"I need a favor."

I look at him like he's lost the last piece of his mind.

"Oh, you need a favor? You storm pass my desk like I've done something to you and now you need me."

"Dee, I am not in the mood for your mouth right now. I need you to handle something."

"Something or somebody?"

"Same difference." He says. "Here, her name is Kelli."

I take the piece of paper with her number and some more information on it.

"Kelli? Why does that name sound familiar?"

"She's the girl from the coffee shop down the way."

"And what exactly am I handling?"

"She went to Thorpe claiming to be pregnant with my baby and has demanded I give her money, a condo and a car or else she'll expose me."

"You know what--"

"No but I am sure you are going to tell me."

"And you are damn right. You are one sad, pathetic piece of a man! You get into all this crap then expect me to make it go away. How do you even know it was her? It could be one of the many other naïve little girls you have on standby."

"I know it was her because she's been calling my phone every day since last week with this pregnancy mess."

"Is there a possibility she could be pregnant?"

"If she is, she needs to find the real baby daddy because it isn't me." He laughs.

"I bet your ass won't be laughing when you get something AJAX can't take off."

"I'm not worried about that. Now, will you handle this for me or not."

"I'll see what I can do, like always."

"Thanks Dee, I appreciate you."

"No, you appreciate what I do for you."

"You know I'll compensate you for your troubles."

"Yea, it'll go right along with the rest of the hush money you deposit every week."

"Woman, stop acting like you aren't enjoying the benefits of this job."

"Benefits? The only one reaping benefits worthy of being mentioned around here is you."

"You know what I mean."

"Clearly I don't."

"Then why do you stay? If I'm such a mess why have you put up with me for ten years?"

"Because no one else can handle you and your shenanigans. Plus, I'm the only admin you can't sleep with and it's not for your lack of trying."

"You do have a point. You are also the only woman I let talk to me this way."

"Does it look like I care? One of these days I won't be here to clean up your mess because I don't know how much more of this I can take."

"You'll be fine."

"Shut up and go home."

He laughs. "You know it is mine and Torre's ten year anniversary tonight."

"Yea and I don't see how she has put up with you this long. I just hope you got her something expensive with all the crap she has to deal with from you."

"You have no idea." He says grabbing his bag and leaving.

Walking back to my desk I start to get angry at the carelessness of this man but I can't because I have no one to blame but myself for me being in this position. Hell, I should have ran the moment I had to sign a confidentiality agreement with Lady Torre Thornton.

"Should have followed your first mind and ran faster than an Olympic Gold Medalist but no you just had to accept the job Daphne!" I scold myself.

I pick up the receiver to dial this trick's number when my office door swings open.

"Can I help you?"

"Yea, you can get up off your ass and get Joseph for me because I know that lying bastard is here!"

Not today devil ... not tuh-day!

Looking around to see who in the name of Jesus this girl is talking too, I turn back to her. "Um, boo you might want to bring it down a notch because this is surely not what you want. Now, what can I do for you?"

"Can you not hear? I need you to get off your ass and do your little assistant job and assist me by getting Joseph out here!"

"Pastor Thornton is not in but if you'd like to leave a message I'd be sure he gets it Ms.--"

"It's Kelli, thank you but I am not leaving until his punk ass talks to me. Joseph, I'm not leaving. You may as well bring your black ass out here. JO-SEPH!" She screams.

I cross my arms and lean back in the chair. She walks over and turns his door knob but it's locked. She begins to beat on it.

"I know your black ass is in there. Come out and face me like a man, punk!"

After a few minutes, she sulks back over to my desk out of breath.

"Are you done?"

"Hell no. Get his ass out here NOW! Deacon Thorpe said he is refusing to give me what I asked for. So, I'm here to tell him, to his face, what I am about to do."

"You decided to tell him what exactly?"

"He can either pay me or I'll tell this whole church and his precious wife everything. And I do mean everything including all the things we've done in here. Oh and how good he is at eating my pu--"

I cut her off. "Kelli is it? I don't know you from a can of paint but what I do know is, you will not stand in my office giving demands. Little girl do you know how many others have stood in the exact same spot, looking just as foolish as you do right now?"

"I don't give a damn about nobody else but me!"

"Well, you should because I can guarantee this ain't the tree you want to come barking around missy. Either you watch that filthy mouth and have a seat for a civilized conversation or you can close my door on your way out and take your chances."

She stands for a minute considering her options before taking the seat in front of my desk.

"Look, I'm sorry but I am sick of being used by Joe. He promised he would pay my rent this month but now he's ignoring my calls. All I want is what he promised me." She says starting to cry. "He said he'd help me."

"Baby, you simple chicks bother my spirit. Here," I say handing her a Kleenex. "I'll give you a minute to get yourself together but this little show you're putting on, it doesn't move me."

She wipes her face and looks at me.

"Oh, did you expect me to feel sorry for you? Girl, you aren't a victim. You knew exactly what you were getting when you backed your narrow ass up on his desk, over the console of his truck or in some hotel room so you will not get any sympathy from me. Now, here's what I can do."

Torre

"I, Torre, take you, Joseph Levi Thornton, to be my lawfully wedded husband, to have and to hold, from this day forward, for better, for worse, for richer, for poorer, in sickness and in health, until death do us part."

"I, Joseph, take you Torre Bea Banks, to be my lawfully wedded wife, to have and to hold, from this day forward, for better, for worse, for richer, for poorer, in sickness and in health, until death do us part."

"Please take the rings and place them on each of your fingers and repeat after me," my pastor said. "With this ring I thee wed, with my body I thee worship, and with all my worldly goods I thee give: In the name of the Father, and of the Son, and of the Holy Ghost. Amen."

"Torre, have you heard a word of what I said?" My momma asks touching my arm.

"I'm sorry momma, I wasn't paying attention. What did you say?" I ask her.

"Chile, where was your mind just now?"

"Nothing, I was just thinking about the day Joseph and I were married. What did you say?"

"I asked if Joseph has anything planned for your anniversary tonight."

"I guess so."

"Well, don't sound so excited about it. What's wrong? Are you feeling okay?" She asks sitting next to me at the table.

"It's nothing momma, I'm just tired I guess."

"Are you sure that's all? You know you can talk to me about anything, right?"

"Yes, I know. It's just..." I start to say before my phone vibrates. I don't have to look to know its Joe calling. I press ignore.

"What were you saying baby?"

"Nothing momma, I'm going to go." I stand, kissing her on the cheek.

"Okay baby but when you're ready to talk, I'll be right here." She says getting up from her chair. "Oh, you didn't forget that tomorrow is family and friends day at our church, did you?"

"No ma'am, I remember."

"You think Joe will mind if you come to service with me? You know everyone would love to see you."

"Of course momma. I'll pick you up and then we can have lunch afterwards."

"I'd like that. Be careful going home."

"I will. Make sure you lock up."

I make it to the car and Joe calls again. I let out a sigh before I hit the phone button on the steering wheel.

"Why haven't you been answering my calls?" He bellows through the phone.

"Joe, you only called once and I was saying goodbye to my mom."

"I don't care who you were talking to, you better answer my call every time. Do you understand?"

"Yes."

"What time are you getting home?" He asks.

"I'm on the way now. What's wrong?"

He doesn't respond before hanging up.

It's takes about 45 minutes to get home from my mom's house. Pulling in the driveway, I see a car parked out front that I don't recognize.

I walk into the house to find candles burning and jazz music playing. I silently pray tonight will be amazing because the last few months have been anything but.

"Joe," I call out. "Joe, where are you?"

When he doesn't answer I put my purse down in the living room and continue to our bedroom. The door is pushed up but not completely closed. I open it and the scene before me stops me dead in my tracks.

"What the hell?"

"Oh my God!" The girl screams before jumping off of Joe.

"You've got to be kidding me," I say. "You lowdown mother--"

"Watch your mouth in my house." He says sitting up in the bed.

"Watch my mouth, are you serious? You're sleeping with some woman in our house, in our bed, on our anniversary and you're telling me to watch my mouth? Screw you Joe!" I scream.

"Look, I don't know what is going on here but I'm leaving." The girl says.

"You're not going anywhere." Joe says to her. "Get your ass back in this bed."

"You're right, she can stay because I'm leaving."

Daphne

This girl is still crying.

I look at my watch. "Baby, are you done because I don't have all night to bother with you. I'm missing the last few episodes of Power and Empire I got recorded."

She sniffs.

"Girl, wipe your face and blow your nose so we can get this conversation over with."

She looks shocked.

"What? Did you think you were the first to ride this ride? Oh girl, you aren't and you will not be the last. So, let's get on with it. First, are you even pregnant?"

"No, that mane doesn't even cum. I told him he needs to get his prostrate checked."

"Too much information sweetie."

"Sorry but no ma'am, ain't no babies coming out of this pus– umm, I mean out of me. I just need some money because I got bills and do you see these nails? I haven't had them done in three weeks."

Lord Jesus where does he find these ratchet heifers.

"Here's what I can do for you." I say placing a document in front of her. "You can sign this confidentiality agreement which comes with a little bit of cash and keep it moving or you can try your luck with Pastor Thornton but I doubt you will get far."

She looks at the document and I already know what she is looking for. I can tell when she lands on it because her eyes light up and her hand quickly grabs the pen I placed beside it.

"Before you sign this, you need to understand what it means. You can never mention your involvement with Pastor Thornton to anyone because if you do, you can be sued. If you start seeing him again, for any reason, there will be no more compensation. This is a one-time benevolent offering, from the church, to help you get on your feet and if you say anything other than this, I'll have the paperwork to prove otherwise. AND if you ever come into my office acting like you've lost your mind, I won't hesitate to knock you on your ass. Understood?"

She nods.

"I need you to say it."

"Yes, I understand."

"Good. Sign here, here, date there and initial there and we are done."

She drops the pen and I reach into my desk drawer and hand her an envelope.

"You be blessed now."

She leaves and I look at the stack of agreements and envelopes I have on hand for times such as this and I shake my head. I file her away in the secret compartment under my desk, with the rest of them before locking it and grabbing the bottle of patron.

Torre

He jumps up, pushing me up against the wall pressing his forearm under my neck.

"Joe, stop! Let me go." I say trying to push his arm from my neck.

"Where do you think you're going?"

"Let me go!"

He removes his arm and steps back. I start to move and he slaps me across the face before grabbing my hair.

Pulling me to him, he whispers through gritted teeth, "I'm only going to tell you this once. Take your ass into the bathroom and shower. You have ten minutes and then I expect you to be in this bed, allowing what's her name--"

"It's Soph--" The girl starts to say,

"I don't care what your name is," Joe spats cutting her off. "Shut up!"

Releasing me, he slings me toward the wall.

"You're so ungrateful. Here I am, giving you an anniversary gift and you throw it in my face."

"This isn't an anniversary gift for me, it's for you but I am not about to sleep with that woman."

He raises his hand.

"Joe, please!"

"Joe, please!" He mimics before walking up to me again. "Do I need to repeat myself?"

I shake my head while tears slide down my face.

"Ten minutes Torre or I'm coming to get you.

I run into the bathroom pushing the door closed. I can't lock it because he has already removed the handle. Looking into the mirror, I see a bruise already forming on my jaw.

"TEN MINUTES!" He yells.

I open my eyes to see light coming through the window. When I move, pain shoots through my body causing me to groan. I sit up realizing I am in the guest room.

I pull my legs up to my chest, remembering last night.

"Do you think I am playing with you? You are an ungrateful slut! Stand in the corner!" Joe's voice plays over and over in my head.

When I refused to participate in Joe's sick game, last night, he forced me to perform oral on the girl. Unsatisfied with that, I had to endure the most degrading sex ever with him. Afterwards, he made me stand in the corner and watch him for almost three hours, with that girl doing everything he could think of.

When she left, he made me sit on my knees next to the bed. I waited until he'd fallen asleep before I ran into the guest bedroom and cried myself to sleep.

I slowly open the door to see if I can hear him, praying he's already left for church. I run across the hall to our bedroom. Seeing the clock on the nightstand I realize I still have time to make it to church with momma.

I go into my closet and grab some clothes to take a shower. Walking out, Joe is sitting on the bed and I jump.

I hug the clothes tight against me because I don't know what mood he's in.

"Torre baby, I'm sorry about last night. I shouldn't have treated you that way. It was our anniversary and I was being selfish. I should have known you'd never go for that type of thing. Can you please forgive me?"

I never look up to face him. He gets up and walks toward me which causes me to flinch.

He places his hand under my chin to raise my head. "Will you please forgive me?"

I don't move.

"After service, I will take you to an early dinner and maybe we can catch that movie you've been wanting to see. How does that sound? It'll be me making up for ruining our anniversary."

"I, uh, I'm going to church with momma, remember. It's their family and friend's day." I stutter.

He lets me go.

"Family and friend's day? Oh ok, it must have slipped my mind. Go ahead."

I don't move because it seems too easy.

"Go ahead and go with your momma. I'll meet you back here when you're done."

I take a step and when he doesn't move, I walk faster to get to the bathroom. Before I make it to the door, he grabs me by the hair, snatching me back.

"JOE!" I scream.

"Did you think I would let you leave here so you can tell your mom all kinds of lies about me?"

"Joe, please! I won't say anything. I just want to spend time with my mom."

He drags me back into the guest bedroom while I fight to get out of his grip.

Getting to the door, he pushes me in. "Get your ass in there and you better not come out. I don't give a damn if you starve to death, you better not move! Am I clear?"

When I don't answer, he moves towards me.

"Yes, I hear you. Please don't hit me again."

"I wouldn't have too if you would learn to keep your mouth and follow directions."

Joseph

"Damn it!" I scream walking back into our bedroom. I stop and look at myself in the mirror before I hear Torre's cellphone vibrating. I look at the screen and it's her mom. I put it on speaker.

"Hey Ma, how are you this morning?"

"Hey Joe, I am doing great. I was calling to see if Torre was on her way to pick me up for church but since you answered her phone, I guess not."

"No ma'am, she's not feeling well. I think it was the seafood she ate last night. I was supposed to call you but I got busy when she started throwing up again."

"Oh no. Well, I'll just come there and take care of her while you go to church."

"No ma'am, you don't have to do that because she's asleep now. I'm only going to

Sunday school and then I'll be back to make sure she is okay. I'll have her call you when she wakes up."

"Are you sure because I don't mind."

"I'm sure and thank you for offering."

"Okay but if she isn't feeling better by tonight, I'll be there."

"Yes ma'am. You have a blessed day now."

I hang up and throw the phone on the bed before going to take a shower.

\- - -

Walking into the church, I am met by Dee.

"Where's Torre?"

"She's not feeling well."

She looks at me.

"What? She has a stomach bug or something."

"I bet she does."

"Dee, I am not in the mood for your shit this morning. I need to get ready for Sunday school."

"No, you need to get ready to repent. Damn spawn of Satan." She says before walking off.

I go into my office and close the door. When I see the Sunday school book on the corner of my desk, I pick it up and throw it across the room.

I press the intercom button. "Dee, have one of the deacons teach my class this morning."

She doesn't respond but I know she heard me. I take a seat at my desk and put my head in my hands before beginning to pray.

I am interrupted by a knock on the door.

"Not now Dee."

"Pastor Thornton?"

"Oh Raven, what can I do for you?"

She smiles before coming in and closing the door.

"I was coming to see if you needed anything this morning."

"No, I think I am good."

"You sure there isn't something I can do for you?" She walks around to the back of my chair, placing her hands on my shoulders. "You look a little stressed."

"I am. Do you have something that can help with that?"

"I might."

I take her hand from my shoulder and pull her around in from of me. "What did you have in mind?" I ask sliding back to let her sit on the end of my desk.

"Whatever you need."

Her eyes travel down to the bulge in my pants.

I rub myself through my pants. "He could use some attention this morning."

She moves from the desk to the couch. I stand and walk over, stopping in front of her. She unzips my pants and takes my penis into her hands before sliding it into her mouth.

"Ah," I moan.

Sound of tapping on the door.

"One second."

"Pastor, I need these--"

I look into Dee's face as she stops at the door.

Raven jumps up, wiping her mouth.

"Dee, shut the door."

She slams it.

"You've got to be freaking kidding me! Of all places, on all days and at all times? Really? You got the nerve to do this now AND WITH HER?"

"I--" Raven begins to say but I stop her.

"Get your nasty ass out of here!" Dee says through clenched teeth.

She rushes out pass Dee who looks at me with disgust written over her face.

"What?" I ask while fixing my pants.

"Is that all you have to say? What is wrong with you?"

"Dee, I don't get in your business, why are you all up in mine?"

"Your business is my business however, getting head when you should be preparing to preach to a congregation of people, who are hungry for God's word is vile. Even for you."

"Isn't that what I was doing, feeding the people?"

"Everything is a joke to you. You are one pitiful ass preacher."

"Gone with all that because I am a damn good preacher and pastor."

"By whose standards because no damn good preacher will be in his office, in God's house, getting head. How can you honestly call yourself a good preacher when you can't help them because you're neck deep in sin?"

"The same as always Dee. I know what I'm doing. Now, why don't you do your job and let me do mine."

"You're absolutely right and from now on, I will but one of these days you're going to wish you'd kept that little thing in your pants."

"Wait, you think my thing is little?"

"I don't know why I even bother to help the unhelpable."

"Is that even a word?"

She throws me the middle finger before turning around.

"Wait Dee. Do you seriously think he is it little?" I ask messing with my pants.

She just looks at me. "I cannot, for the life of me, figure out what goes through your simple mind sometimes. You have a beautiful wife at home who loves you yet you treat her like crap. She's probably at home right now, covering up another bruise from the one man who vowed to love and protect her. And instead of trying to get help, you're here getting head."

"Wow Dee. Maybe you should preach this morning."

"Go to hell." She says before storming out.

I walk behind my desk just as my cellphone is vibrating with a call from my ex-wife Carmen.

"What's up Carmen?"

"I need to see you?"

"Not today, I have too much going on."

"Please Joe, I really need you."

"I'll call you after service."

Daphne

As I round the corner, I run right into Sis. Thorpe or Raven.

"Daphne, can I speak with you for a moment."

"Nope." I say, trying to walk pass her.

"Please, it'll only take a minute."

"What?"

"Um," she says looking around before lowering her voice. "Can you keep what you saw between us? I don't want this getting back to my husband."

"Are you serious?"

"Please. I don't need him to find out."

I step a little closer to her, "You wouldn't have to worry about that if you were to keep your mouth to yourself."

"I know and I'm sorry. I didn't mean for it to happen."

"Oh, let me guess, you fell on it?"

"You don't have to get smart with me, I said I was sorry." She says folding her arms.

"Yes you are but that's not my problem. Now, if you'd excuse me."

"You know what, forget you, Ms. High and Mighty. I don't know why I said something to you in the first place. It's not like you'll say anything that can potentially hurt your precious pastor. Besides, all I have to do is say the word and have my husband fire you."

"Your husband, head of the deacon board, husband? The same husband who has tried to eat my cookies on several occasions. That husband?"

I chuckle before stepping closer to her. "Look heifer, you aren't in any position to threaten me. You must have forgotten that I'm the Pastor's Admin which means I know this isn't the first time you've had your lips locked around his cock. So please, puh-lez, do me the favor of telling your husband because I can guarantee the day you do will be one deacon meeting you wouldn't want to miss."

"I'm not scared of you."

"Well, play your hand Little Miss Muppet and we shall see but may I suggest for you to reshuffle your cards because I know the hand I'm playing with. What about you?"

"I don't have time for this." She says.

"No correction, I don't have time for this so next time, think twice before coming for me. I am the one thou shall call to pray with, not the one to play with. Have a great day now."

I leave her standing there as I grab my purse from my desk. I drive over to the Thornton house and let myself in.

"Torre," I call out. "Torre, baby, where are you?"

I check the master bedroom but she isn't there. I open the door to the guest room and she's crouched in the corner. When she raises her head, my heart drops.

I rush over to her.

"Come on and let's get you cleaned up."

I take her into the bathroom and turn on the shower. I help her get undressed and she gets in and closes the door.

After she finishes, I wrap the towel around her and she cries into my shoulder.

"Why does he keep doing this?" She asks.

"I don't know."

I lead her to the bedroom.

"Lay down while I get you something for pain or you can pack a bag and come home with me."

She shakes her head and I shake mine before going into the kitchen.

I fix her a grill cheese sandwich along with a few grapes before grabbing a bottle of water from the refrigerator and two Naproxen pills from the linen closet.

"Sit up so you can eat and take these."

She slowly drags herself up.

"Take a few bites first so this medicine doesn't make you sick."

"Sicker than I already am?" She asks.

"You don't have to stay here."

"Where will I go Dee?"

"You have me and your mom."

"NO! My mom cannot know about this. It's embarrassing enough that you do."

"Why do you let him treat you like shit? He respects everybody else except the wife who shares his bed. Why Torre?"

"I don't know why he does it."

"That's not what I mean? Why do you let him treat you like this? You don't deserve it and you damn sure don't have to take it."

"I love him."

"Baby girl, love doesn't hurt."

"Can you just give me the pills? I need to sleep."

"Sure. I'll leave you alone but just know I'm here for you."

Torre

I open my eyes to see Joe sitting next to the bed. I jump pulling the comforter closer to me.

"I'm not going to hurt you." He says sliding his chair closer. "I am so sorry Torre. For last night and for this morning. Can you please forgive me?"

I don't move or say anything. He grabs my arm and I flinch in pain.

"I did this to you." He lays his head down on my arm and cries. "Say you won't leave me. Please Torre, I cannot lose you."

"What did I do?"

He raises up and looks at me.

"What did I do to deserve this? I thought you said you loved me."

"I do love you and this isn't your fault. It's mine but I promise you, I'll never lay another hand on you."

I look at him.

"I promise. Will you forgive me?"

"Yeah, I forgive you."

He stands and picks me up into his arms, carrying me into our bathroom where he has a bath ran.

Standing me on the floor, he removes the robe. Tears are rolling down my face so he takes his hands to wipe them.

"Don't cry. I promise I won't hurt you again. Take a bath while I finish preparing dinner. When you're ready, come to the dining room and eat." He kisses me on the cheek before leaving.

I listen for him to close the door before I let out the breath I'd been holding. I step into the tub and allow the warmness of the water to sooth my aching body. I can tell he used Epson Salt because I can feel the grains on the floor of the tub. He learned it was good for soreness after the first few times he abused me.

I pull my knees up to my chest and I cry.

"Dear God, please forgive me." I silently pray. "Forgive me for stepping outside of your will. Forgive me for forfeiting all the times you told me to move and I stood still. Please hear my prayer and show me what you will have me to do. Amen."

I sit in the tub until the water turns cold. Getting out, I dry off before putting back on my robe with nothing else underneath. I walk over to the sink and brush my hair up into a ponytail before brushing my teeth and washing my face.

I slowly walk into the dining room to find the table filled with candles, flowers and his usual apology meal of salmon and rice.

There's a gift on my side of the table which is another one of his apology tactics. I am willing to bet, it is probably the bracelet to the necklace he bought last week.

Sitting at the table he comes in, smiling and I cringe.

"Hey, I was about to come and check on you. How are you feeling?"

"Better."

"Good. Look baby," he says kneeling beside me, "I am so sorry about the last couple of days. I've been so stressed with stuff at the church but I should not have taken it out on you. I won't allow that to happen again. Do you believe me?"

I nod.

"Thank you baby." He says kissing me on the top of the head. "Open your gift while I go and get your plate." He says walking into the kitchen.

"Oh, I got your favorite, Pralines and Cream ice cream for dessert."

I open the box and it was just what I thought.

"Do you like the bracelet? It matches your necklace."

"Yes, thank you."

He sits the plate in front of me, kissing me on the jaw.

We eat in silence for the next thirty minutes. Then I sit and watch him clean the kitchen before we go upstairs for makeup sex.

The usual routine.

Joseph

It's been a few weeks since Torre and I made up. Everything has been going great, at home and at church. I haven't heard anymore from Kelli which lets me know Dee has done her job.

I leave the office headed home but I decide to make a stop first. Pressing call on the Bluetooth, my soldier stands at the sound of her voice.

"Ginger speaking."

"Hey, can you fit me in today."

"Of course, anything for you daddy. Are you on the way?"

"I'll be there in ten minutes."

"The door will be open."

I pull into the parking garage and get out. I take the elevator to the top floor before walking into her condo, closing then locking the door. I head to her massage room and find her standing there waiting.

She seductively watches me as I undress.

"Lay down daddy and let me take care of you."

I do as she says, getting comfortable on her table. She doesn't bother to cover me with a sheet because we wouldn't need it.

She puts on some soft music before covering my chest and stomach with massage oil. As her hands roam, my soldier stands at full attention, throbbing for her attention.

She smiles.

Moving to the end of the table, her hands move from my ankles to my shins and then up to my thighs. She spreads my legs, climbing onto the table, in between them on her knees.

Her hands find their way to my hard erection, she is now massaging.

"Um, yea, just like that." I moan, closing my eyes.

I feel her lips on the tip as my hand moves to the back of her head.

I raise up on my elbows to watch her. I like to see and hear her gag while the combination of our juices fall from her mouth.

"Yea, take it all." I say as I push her head down.

When she comes up for air, I beckon for her to come to me.

"Is that good daddy?"

"Yes," I reply before I suck her tongue into my mouth while she slides down onto me.

"Ahh," she moans as I hold her in place inserting every inch. "Hmm, yes, give it to me."

"Is this what you want?"

"Um, yeah." She moans.

I release her as she sits up and begins to ride, fast then slow. I grab her by the waist and pump into her as she cries out in pleasure.

"Oh, I cumming." She screams bucking like a wild horse. "Oh, shit!"

She moves down and takes me in her mouth as I explode all over her face.

"Damn girl. You're getting better each time."

"Did I make you happy?"

"Yes, daddy is really happy. Now, get a towel to clean me up."

As soon as she leaves the room, my watch notifies me of an incoming call from my wife.

I answer it as she comes back into the room. I signal for her to be quiet while the call connects. She smiles while walking towards me.

"Hey baby, are you ok?" I ask.

"Yes, I was trying to see where you are. Daphne said you'd already left the church."

Before I could answer, Ginger was kneeling in front of me, licking on my now semi-soft erection.

"Um, yea, I'll be there in about 30 minutes. Is everything alright?"

"We're supposed to do dinner, remember?"

"Yea."

"Is everything alright with you?"

"I, oh--"

"What are you doing?" She snaps.

"I stopped for a massage."

"Oh, is that what you're calling it now? You know what, you are a piece of work."

"Torre, you better watch your mouth talking to me."

"Or what Joe? I cannot believe your audacity. You--"

"I, uh, shit!" I say before I could stop myself.

"You know what, screw you. I will not be here when you get back." Torre screams before releasing the call.

I look at my watch to make sure the call ended before I grab Ginger's head and begin thrusting into her mouth.

I hold her in place until I release down her throat. Pulling her up to me, I kiss her on the lips.

"You are a nasty girl."

"Anything for you."

"I have to go but I'll leave your money up front."

Daphne

I roll my eyes when I see Joe's picture pop up on my phone's screen. I press answer and then the speaker button.

"What's up Joe?"

"Where is Torre?"

"Hello to you too."

"Dee, I don't have time to play with you. Where is Torre?"

"I pray she's on her way to starting a new life without you."

"Why can't you just answer the damn question? Have you seen my wife or not?" He yells.

"First of all you need to lower your voice. Second of all, had you been home instead of doing only God knows what, you wouldn't have to be searching for her. Your ass scared aren't you?" I laugh.

"I should have known you wouldn't give me a straight answer. One of these days your smart mouth is going to get you--"

"Ooh wee what pastor cock-um-down? Is it going to get me embarrassed, talked about, lied on or judged? Because all those things come with being your admin anyway."

"Never mind Daphne. One damn question always turns into a freaking sermon with you."

"Well, at least one of us is preaching the good news."

"Have a great rest of your night." He says before releasing the call.

"Yea, you better find somebody else to play with because I am not thee one!" I say to the phone's blank screen before I go to refill my glass of wine.

Walking back into the living room, the doorbell rings. I open it.

"Torre?"

"Dee, can I come in?"

"Of course." I say stepping back. "You want something to drink? Water, juice, wine or--"

"Can I have a glass of wine?"

I stop and look at her because I've never seen her drink.

"Wine, are you sure?"

"No, it just sounded good but I'll take some water."

"Water it is." I say walking into the kitchen.

I come out too see her sitting on the floor, in front of the couch, with her shoes off.

"Who are you and what have you done with Torre?"

She smiles. "This is a little fancy for water, don't you think?" She says referring to the wine glass I hand her.

"Just because you don't drink, it doesn't mean you can't look like it. Now, what's up with you? Are you on the run?"

"I'm tired Dee." She sighs.

"Oh," I say sitting my glass on the table before sliding next to her on the floor.

"What did Joe do now? You know he called right before you showed up?"

"You didn't tell him I was here, did you?" She asks, sitting up.

"Calm down, you know I wouldn't do that, you are always safe here. Besides, you weren't here when he called so technically, I did not have anything to tell him."

She relaxes.

"I don't know what to do Dee because I am really, really tired."

"Torre, a person who is really, really tired seeks rest and leaving home for an hour isn't it."

"I shouldn't have come here." She says getting up.

"Girl, sit your ass down and drink that water."

"I just don't want to be attacked by you, I get enough of that at home."

"Baby, the attack is what happens when your husband blacks your eyes. What this is, here and now, is me being genuinely concerned."

She starts to cry. "I don't know what to do. He didn't always act like this." She says wiping her face. "I used to think he loved me but now, I don't even recognize who he is."

"What changed?"

"He started his own church. The success and the women throwing themselves at him turned him into a monster behind closed doors."

"You stay though. Why?"

"You wouldn't understand."

I laugh. "How do you know? You assume because I look well put together that I wouldn't understand what it is like to live with a monster?"

"I didn't mean--"

"When I was 19, my mom passed away from colon cancer. She was diagnosed and dead in six months. Losing her changed my life because although I was 19 and she left me a small insurance policy, I didn't know the first thing about being on my own."

"Dee, I don't want to sound inconsiderate but losing your mom is not comparable to getting my ass beat."

I roll my eyes before continuing. "Momma had this best friend name Beatrice and I loved that woman. She was like a second mother to me so when my mom died, I didn't think twice about letting her move in with me, she was there all the time anyway. To make a very long story short, Beatrice took advantage of me."

"How?"

"She popped my lesbian cherry and girl, that woman was a beast with her mouth. She would do things to me that made my toes curled."

I look at Torre and her mouth is open.

"But there was something else she was good at, lying. I didn't know it but she and my mom had been lovers since college."

"Wait, what?" Torre says.

"Yep. She got drunk one night and begin to tell me everything."

"You never suspected your mom was gay?"

"Nev-ver! Not even a clue because she and my mom didn't even look at each other like that. I never saw them be intimate, flirty towards one another or anything so of course it blew my mind when I found out but I was in love by then."

"Wow! Is that why you like women?"

"I guess you can say that because I've never been with a man. I told you I was 19 and she took full advantage of it. She made me forget all about a man. She was good and I didn't know any better so whatever she asked me to do, I did until one day I didn't."

"What happened?"

"I got tired. She had me at her beck & call and she knew it. She would have me doing things like giving her oral sex in the middle of the day, in the car while in a grocery store parking lot. One time, we almost got caught having sex in a park because she wanted it and wouldn't take no for an answer. That was it for me. I was damn tired so I asked her to leave."

"Did she?"

I shake my head no. "That would be the day she became my abuser."

I stop when I feel myself getting emotional. Torre touches my arm.

"I was afraid of her and she knew it. She made my life a living hell, even in the house I owned. Torre, she was so bad that if she came home after having a bad day at work, if I left dishes in the sink, if I came home late or looked at her wrong; she would punish me. One night, I hung out with some coworkers and didn't come in until after midnight. The house was dark so I assumed she was asleep. I had installed a lock on my door by then but I was tipsy from hanging out and forgot to lock it before I went to sleep. Needless to say, I woke up to her handcuffing me to the bed. For twelve hours, she burned me with cigarettes, sodomized me with a dildo and beat me with a belt."

"Oh Dee. Why didn't you leave?"

"The same reason you don't, fear. And I would fall for the sweet sounding apologies and the puppy dog eyes when she promised to never do it again. The final straw was coming home to find she'd created a punishment room in the basement with handcuffs, gags and that type of shit. I still have scars."

"How did you get out?"

"Death intervened. She left the house going to work, one morning and not five minutes later, her car was hit by an eighteen wheeler and she burned alive. It was the best day of my life. So when you say I don't understand, you are wrong."

"You got a way out. I still have to go home to my abuser and every time, after he promises not to do it again, gets worse."

"You do have a way out Torre, you just have to take it. But as much as I want you to survive, you are the only person who can decide when you've had enough."

"It's not that easy." She says lowering her head.

"Why not? All you have to do is pack your shit and move. What is he going to do? It's not like y'all have children or anything."

"I'm pregnant." She blurts.

The words to reply get caught in my throat. "Whoa, I did not see that coming. When did you find out?"

"Yesterday. I went to Walmart, got a pregnancy test and took it in the women's bathroom."

"Does Joe know?"

She shakes her head.

"Child, I'm going to need something stronger than this damn wine."

Joseph

Walking into my office the next morning, I am met by Raven.

"Sister Thorpe, what can I do for you this morning?"

"Good morning Pastor, can we talk?"

"Sure." I unlock my office door and let her walk in first. "If this is about Dee, you don't have to worry because she's not going to say anything."

"I'm not concerned about her."

"What is it then?"

"Last night, I overheard my husband on the phone talking to one of the other deacons about a young lady who says she's pregnant by you."

"And?"

"Is this true? Are you sleeping with someone else in the church?"

"Are you serious?"

"Very. Joe, are you sleeping with someone else besides me?"

"Get out of my office."

"I'm not going anywhere until you answer me. Are you sleeping with somebody else, in this church, besides me?" She yells.

I walk up to her and before she can react, I grab her by the throat.

"First of all, lower your got damn voice. Secondly, you and I never slept together. You gave me head, which you're not that good at." I say pushing her away from me. "Get out of my office Raven."

She gasp and grabs her neck.

"I cannot believe you did that."

"And I cannot believe you're standing in my office with this crap. I have enough to deal with, like your meddling ass husband."

"All I want to know--"

I turn back to her so fast that she jumps.

"Raven, please leave my office."

"I LOVE YOU!" She screams.

"You love who? You better say Jesus because I know it's not me."

"You. I love you." She cries. "I know I am not suppose too but I do. My husband is so wrapped up in the business of this church until he forgets he has a wife but you, when you look at me I see the love in your eyes."

I laugh. "Baby, that's lust and as old as you are, you should know the difference between them by now. Do you not pay attention in bible study?"

She cries harder.

"Go home and make things right with your husband because I don't love you and I would hate for you to lose everything, you've worked all these years for, over whatever you have conjured up in your head." I say sitting behind my desk.

"Why are you being so mean?"

"Did you not hear what I said? You gave me head, twice, which does not constitute love. Look Raven, do yourself a favor and go home to your husband before I have to fire him."

She wipes her face. "Just so you know, some of the deacons are planning an emergency church meeting."

"For what?"

"Your job."

"Well tell your husband I said good luck. Now, close my door on your way out."

When I don't hear the door close, I look up to see Dee.

"How long have you been there?"

"Long enough." She says shaking her head.

"Where is my wife?"

I roll my eyes. "I don't know. Now, what did old girl want? Is there something else you've done that I need to take care of?"

"Thorpe and a few deacons are calling for an emergency church meeting to have me terminated."

"Well, it was only a matter of time."

"Whose side are you on?"

"I'm on the Lord's side." She says.

"Very funny Dee."

"What are you going to do?"

"Nothing. Their schemes will not work because my congregation loves me."

"Your congregation?"

"Yep. Now, can you call my wife and let her know I expect her to be home tonight or she can find somewhere else to stay?"

"Maybe she should." She says walking out.

When Dee leaves, I turn on my computer and pull up the by-laws of the church.

Later that evening, I walk in to find Torre coming down the hall.

"Where have you been?"

"I went to see my mom and then I stopped by the store. Dinner will be ready in ten minutes."

She walks pass me like she didn't stay out all night. I take two deep breathes before dropping my bag in the chair and heading into the bathroom to wash my hands.

When I get to the table, she is walking out with two plates, sitting one in front of me.

"What is this?"

"It's a new jerk chicken pasta. I thought–"

"You thought?"

"Joe, I thought you'd like this new recipe. That's all." She says.

I swipe the plate off the table before I grab her by the hair.

"Joe, please stop. I'm sorry, I'll make something else."

"Bitch, you're always sorry but tonight I'm going to show you who's the man of this house. Did you think you could just leave and stay out all night without any consequences? DID YOU?"

"I'm sorry. I just went to Dee's."

I drag her into the master bedroom and throw her against the bed.

"Strip."

"Joe--"

"Are you hard of hearing?"

"JOE! Please stop, I'm pregnant."

I take a step back. "You're what?"

"I'm pregnant."

"You lying slut! Whose baby is it?"

"What? Why would you ask me that?"

"I know it's not mine so whose baby is it? Is that where you were last night, spending time with your baby daddy?"

"You know I'm not cheating on you."

"LIAR!" I take off my belt and begin hitting her over and over. When I am too tired to swing, I drop the belt.

I stand over her breathing hard. "You need to learn your place."

She doesn't say anything.

"I have a meeting and when I get back I want a real dinner on the table. Do you understand?"

When she doesn't answer, I take a step toward her. I push her but she doesn't answer.

"Torre."

She doesn't respond. I check her pulse.

"No, no!" I say to myself walking in circles. I grab my phone. "Dee, I need your help."

Daphne

I rush into the house to find Joe pacing.

"What happened? Where is Torre?"

"She will not wake up."

"What? Where is she?"

"Dee--"

"Joe, where the fuck is Torre?" I yell.

"She's in the bedroom."

I run down the hall, to the master bedroom

to find Torre on the floor beside the bed.

"Torre, baby wake-up. Torre."

"Is she dead?" Joe ask from the door.

"No and you better thank God. Call 911."

"I can't Dee, do you know how bad this will look?"

"Does it look like I care about your image? CALL 911 NOW!"

"Can't you just take her to the hospital if I put her in your car?"

"You are a lowdown, dirty, good for nothing piece of shit."

I pat my pockets for my phone, realizing I left it in the car. I get up and run outside.

"911, what is your emergency?"

"Um, my friend will not wake up."

"Is she breathing?"

"Yes ma'am."

"What happened to her?"

"I don't know, I found her on the floor of her bedroom."

"What is her name?"

"Ma'am, her name is Torre Thornton and the address is 1001 Fen Bark Hollow in Cordova. I will answer any additional questions, you have, but can you please send an ambulance first."

"One is in route. Now, tell me your name?"

"Daphne Gary."

"Ms. Gary, does Torre have any medical conditions?" The operator asks.

"No but she's pregnant."

"How far along is she?"

"I don't know."

"Are you with her?"

I walk back into the bedroom. When I kneel next to her she moves.

"Oh my God, she's waking up. Torre, can you hear me?"

"Dee," she cries. "Dee."

"I'm here. Stay still, the paramedics are on the way."

"No, no paramedics." She whines.

"Torre, you need to be taken to the hospital."

"Ma'am, is she okay?" The operator asks.

"Yes, she's waking up but she's still groggy."

"The ambulance is pulling in. Is the door open?"

"I hear them and yes it's open."

"Okay, you can disconnect the call now."

A few minutes later, the paramedics come in. I move to allow them to kneel next to Torre, who is now sitting beside the bed.

"Ma'am, can you hear me?"

"Yes." She answers.

"Can you tell me what happened?"

"I, um, I passed out."

"Have you ever passed out before?" One of the EMTs asks.

"No but I think it's because I haven't had anything to eat. I'm fine now."

"Can we at least check your vitals?"

"Sure but I don't want to be transported."

"Torre, you need to go to the hospital." I tell her.

"I'm fine. They can check my vitals and that's it."

The EMTs check her out but because she is refusing to go to the hospital, they have her sign a form and then leave.

I walk back into the bedroom to find her sitting on the bed. Joe has now reappeared.

"Dee—"

"Save it Joe! What is it going to take for you to get your head out of your ass? You almost killed this damn girl tonight and she won't even take her crazy ass to the hospital. What the fuck is wrong with y'all?"

Torre is crying and Joe looks like a deer caught in headlights.

"You know what, you two fools deserve each other."

Torre

It's been a week since Joe's latest tantrum left me, again, battered and bruised. When I finally woke up, Dee was there. She'd called the paramedics but I couldn't risk going to the hospital and Joe being arrested.

I haven't seen my mom because I don't want her to see the bruises so Joe lied and told her I'd gone away to some women's retreat.

He's very good at lying. I guess you can say I am too.

I am sitting at my vanity when he comes into the bathroom.

"Torre, can we talk?"

I nod.

"Look, I am so sorry for the way I treated you last week."

"Just last week?"

"Please hear me out. When you passed out, I thought I'd killed you--"

"I wish you had."

"Don't say that." He says kneeling next to me.

"Why not? It's not like you care."

"Baby, I do care and I love you."

"This isn't love Joe. Look at my face, my legs, my arm; this is not love. What did I do to deserve this?"

"It's not you--"

"It is me!" I yell getting up from the vanity. "It's me that's being beaten, every time you get upset. It is me living this nightmare. So don't say it isn't me when it is. WHAT DID I DO?"

He stands up but doesn't say anything.

"You treat everybody else better than you treat your wife. I've never disrespected you, never cheated on you and never lied to you yet I'm the one who is being tormented. Me! The same person who is here when you need someone to pray over you. The same person who loves even the fleshly part of you when everybody else gets the man in the pulpit. I am the one who knows your demons and I still love you. Why do I deserve this?"

"You didn't do anything. I'm the one who has to fix this."

"You keep saying that but I always end up with more scars to cover."

"Okay Torre, I get it."

"You don't because you're killing me Joe."

"I said I was sorry. I know I've made promises before but I will never lay another hand on you."

I don't respond.

"Once we get this church meeting over with and the Love Banquet done, how about we get away for a while."

"Whatever Joe."

"Torre baby," he says walking up to me causing me to take a step back.

He raises his hands and walks closer. "I make a vow to never hurt you again." He says kissing me on the jaw.

I close my eyes and stand there. I feel him turn to leave.

"Oh, I'll have Dee make you an appointment."

I open my eyes and look at him. "What kind of appointment?"

"For the abortion. It'll have to be out of town because you know how folk talk in this city."

My hand instantly goes to my stomach.

"I'm not having an abortion."

"Torre, you know how I feel about children. I don't want any and I have made that perfectly clear."

"Well, it seems God had other plans."

"He has his and I have mine. I'll see you at the church."

I sit back at the vanity. I don't know why I am stunned at his words because it's the typical Joe. I shake my head, grab the makeup brush and begin the process of putting on the face of the doting wife.

I pull into the parking lot of the church and it is packed. Once I park and get out, Daphne is waiting for me at the door.

"Wow Dee, there are more people here tonight than on Sundays."

"Thorpe is pulling out all the stops for tonight's meeting." She says drily.

"Are you okay?" I ask her.

"You ready?" Joe asks, walking up and taking my hand without giving Dee a chance to answer. I plaster on a smile as we and the rest of the ministerial staff walk into the sanctuary to take our seats.

"Now that Pastor Thornton is here, this meeting is now called to order." Deacon Thorpe's voice booms over the mic. "Order."

The talking ceases as he raises the mic again. "This is an emergency meeting called in regards to vacating the position currently held by Pastor Joseph Thornton."

An uproar begins.

"Order!" He yells out. "If we can't have a civilized meeting, we will adjourn and place the vote into the hands of the deacons and trustees."

"What gives you the authority to call this meeting?" Missionary Caldwell screams.

"As I stated, some deacons and members of this church have asked for this meeting regarding the position currently held by Joseph Thornton."

"This is some bull." She yells.

"Sis. Caldwell, please give us a chance to fully explain the situation." Deacon Harper says.

She takes her seat as they continue.

"Before we begin, let us have a word of prayer." Deacon Harper states. "Father God, in

Heaven, it is once again your humble servant petitioning your throne. God, we come tonight to ask you to guide this meeting. Do by your power what is right and just. Do by your power what man cannot. Lead us in the right direction for we don't know what you have in store but we trust your will. Bind our tongues so that no evil can be spoken and cover our minds so that evil cannot prevail. You are the head of this house and we call on you to lead us. Amen."

"Amen." Those gathered say in unison.

He nods at Deacon Thorpe to continue.

"As it has been stated, some of the members have asked for Pastor Thornton's resignation, effective immediately."

"On what grounds?" A member yells out.

"Conduct unbecoming of a pastor."

The members all start talking for a second time.

"Order!"

As they begin to quiet down, Deacon Thorpe speaks again.

"Section 2a of our church bylaws states, 'The Pastor's chief duties are to feed and lead the church in carrying out God's will as it is written in I Peter 5:1-4. More specifically, he is to preach, teach, train, model Christian character and lead in worship on a regular basis.' If he can't do this, the members have a right to ask for him to be terminated. As further stated by the bylaws, section--"

"We don't want to hear about no freaking bylaws. We are not getting rid of our pastor! You have been after him since you got here." A member screams out.

"With all due respect, this is not personal. As a standing deacon in this church, it is our responsibility to ensure the members and governing body are being led by someone capable of holding the position. I understand some of you may be upset but it is up to all the members of this church to decide if and when he is not." Deacon says. "The bylaws state, in section five the pastor can be terminated by 2/3rds the members of the church."

"Then let's vote because this is not right. That man started this church." Another member jumps up and says.

"He may have started it but it is God's house."

"Mane you with some mess so stop all that talking and let's vote." Someone yells causing some members to laugh.

"Very well." Deacon Harper replies. "I need all of you to listen. In order to vote, you must be an active member of the congregation. Stationed at each ballot box is someone who can verify your right standing within the church. You will need to provide identification before you will be given a ballot and you can only receive one ballot per person. Once you're done, place it in one of the boxes located on each side of the altar."

"Y'all act like we're voting for president." Someone yells.

"Who's going to count the votes?"

"We have two members of the city council here who will review and count them."

"We don't trust them no more than we trust you." Mother Marshall says causing the church to erupt in laughter again.

"Mother Marshall, we can assure you we only want the best for the church."

"If you did, we wouldn't be here." She counters.

After almost an hour and half, everyone has cast their vote. We are now sitting around waiting for them to be counted.

I see Dee walk out so I follow her.

"Dee, are you ok?"

"I'm good Torre."

"Look, I know you're still upset about what happened and I'm sorry."

"What are you sorry for?"

I don't say anything.

"When are you going to stop covering for him? You should have his ass to jail when you had the chance."

"I couldn't."

"You could have, you chose not to. I pray the next time it won't be the baby."

"Joe didn't tell you?" I ask.

"Tell me what?"

"He wants me to have an abortion."

"And I bet you're going to do it too."

"Dee, I'm keeping my baby and if that means leaving him, so be it."

"We shall see."

"I know it may not seem like it but I really appreciate you Daphne."

"Thank you for your appreciation but I'd much rather have you safe and alive. Can you do that by choosing you for a change?"

"I will. I promise."

She hugs me.

"I'm going into my office to lie down. Will you come and get me before the results are read."

Daphne

It's going on ten o'clock when Councilman Waterman finally announce all the votes have been counted.

I rise to go and wake Torre but Joe nods for me not too.

"What are the results? Some of us have to work tomorrow." Missionary Caldwell says.

"Based on the votes tonight, Pastor Thornton will retain his position as Pastor of Assembly of God Christian Center."

Cheers sound out as he stands to greet the members. Some of the deacons are pissed as they grab their things to go. I can't blame them.

When Pastor Thornton looks over at me, I shake my head before I leave to let Torre know.

By the time I make it to her office, I see Deacon Thorpe going in. I rush over to the door, he left cracked to listen in.

"Deacon Thorpe, from the look on your face, I am guessing the church decided to keep my husband." She says.

"Unfortunately."

"So, what can I do for you?"

"You can get your husband to resign."

"You know he's not going to do that."

"He doesn't deserve to be a pastor. We all know this position is a joke to him."

"You're wrong Deacon Thorpe. Joe loves this church. It doesn't excuse what he does in his personal life but we both know the membership has tripled since the first year."

"Yea and so have the complaints."

"Deacon Thorpe, I can't help the allegations that are being made about my husband. All I know is, this church is doing better than it has ever done and according to the votes tonight, the members agree."

"It doesn't make it right. He needs to resign!" He says raising his voice.

Hearing him get loud, I push the door open. "Is everything alright?"

"Yes, Deacon Thorpe was just leaving."

"You all can act like you don't know what's going on but you won't always be able to cover for him." He says looking from me to Torre.

"Deacon Thorpe, I understand you're upset--"

"You're damn right and you are partly to blame."

"Me?" I ask.

"Yes, you're a willing accomplice in all of this. You cover for him, shielding his faults and for what? I know he pays you well but come on Daphne. How much longer will the money be worth it before it becomes too much for you?"

"You need to leave." I say to him.

"I'm leaving but I want you to know that you will never find happiness as long as you are connected to him. Good night ladies."

"What was that about?" I ask Torre acting like I wasn't listening.

"He wants me to convince Joe to resign."

"That'll never happen."

"We both know that."

"You both know what?" Joe asks coming in.

"Nothing, take your wife home. It has been a long day." I tell him.

The next day, I get to the church to enjoy the peace Saturday morning brings. I begin sorting through the mail from yesterday when I see a letter from the Memphis Health Department.

"Oh God! Should I open it? Yes, you open all his mail." I say having a full conversation with myself. I open the letter and reading the words cause my throat to burn. Good Lord, what has this man gotten into now?

"Dear Joseph Thornton,

It is very imperative you contact us concerning a very urgent health matter. Please call our office as soon as possible. If we do not hear from you, a certified letter will be sent to your home address."

I grab the phone from my desk and dial his number.

"What's up Dee, why are you in the office on a Saturday?"

"Where are you?"

"Headed to the store for Torre, what's wrong?"

"We need to talk, can you come by the church?"

"Can it wait?"

"If it could, I wouldn't have called."

"Fine, I am on my way."

Twenty minutes later, he comes in whistling.

"What's so urgent?"

"This," I say handing him the letter.

When he finishes, he looks up at me. "What does this mean?"

"How in the hell should I know. What or should I say, who have you been doing?"

"Nobody."

"We both know that's a lie."

"Look, put it on my desk and I will take care of it."

"That's it?" I ask.

"Yea, what else? Is there something more?"

"No but aren't you worried?"

"Why should I be? God has me covered." He laughs.

"Are you seriously laughing at this?"

"Dee, it's nothing. I will call them Monday morning. Now go home and get laid or go have a drink because the last thing you need to do is spend another Saturday closed up in your office." He says turning to walk out but stops.

"Oh, I need you to find a clinic for Torre."

"What kind of clinic?"

"Abortion."

"What? Why? Is something wrong?"

"Yes, I don't want any children."

"Are you seriously being selfish right now? After everything you've put that woman through, you're really going to ask her to have an abortion?"

"I'm not asking, I'm telling. She knew how I felt before we got married."

"Just when I think you couldn't get any more disgusting."

"Whatever Dee, just get it done."

Joseph

"What the hell have I done?" I ask myself when I get to the truck replaying the words found on that piece of paper. "SHIT!" I say hitting the steering wheel before laying my head back on the seat.

My phone rings bringing me out of my thoughts. I answer it without looking at the caller id.

"This is Joseph Thornton."

"Joe, are you really going to act like I didn't call you weeks ago?"

"Carmen?"

"You know it's me. I need to see you."

"I can't right now, I have too much going on."

"Joe, please."

"I can't but I'll call you in a few hours."

"Joe--"

I hang up without giving her a chance to convince me. I go by the store to get the things Torre asked for. Pulling up, at home, it feels like a weight drops in my spirit.

I park in the garage and sit there for over twenty minutes as all kinds of thoughts go through my head. Images of me hitting Torre makes me sick at the stomach. "I am a monster who abuses his wife. I lie and cheat acting like I cannot be dealt with by God and now, the health department." I say out loud. "What have I done?"

I grip the steering wheel until I feel the leather getting hot to the inside of my hands. "God, please forgive me. I hope it is not too late to fix this."

After another few minutes, I go inside and put the bags on the kitchen's island. I walk into the living room to see Torre laying on the couch asleep. I go over and sit in front of her.

For a few minutes I watch her. Then I reach over and touch her face. When she opens her eyes, she jumps up.

"Babe, calm down."

"You scared me."

"I'm sorry, I didn't mean too. You were sleeping so peacefully that I didn't want to wake you."

"Joe--"

"No Torre listen." I say getting emotional, falling on my knees in front of her. "I have messed everything up."

She removes the blanket and turns her body toward me. I lay my head in her lap.

"I am so sorry for all the pain you've had to endure because of me. I had no right to treat you the way I have when you didn't deserve it. Please forgive me."

She rubs my head as she rocks back and forth.

"I need you Torre. Will you please forgive me? Will you please stay with me? I promise I am going to get the help I need."

I raise my hands and wrap them around her stomach. "I don't want you to have an abortion. I was being mean and selfish. We can make this work."

She covers my hand with hers and I feel her tears.

I look up at her.

"Just say you'll stay. Please Torre, I love you."

"I love you too Joe but I'm tired."

She releases me and sits back on the couch, pulling her legs up to her chest.

I sit on the floor with my back against the table. "You have every right to be and I know I'm asking a lot but will you please give me a chance to make it right?"

"What's different this time?"

"I realized just how big of a fool I've been. When I pulled in the driveway, just now, God begin replaying some of the things I've done and it was like a horror movie. I don't even know who I am anymore."

She starts to say something but stops.

"Torre, I promise not to get upset at you for being honest. Truth is, I don't blame you for wanting to leave. After everything I have put you through, you should run and never look back but

I am begging you to give me one more chance. If I don't keep my promise, this time, I'll leave."

"I hear you Joe but I also know you and I'm afraid. While you are sitting here looking and sounding like my husband, we both know the demon within you can rear its ugly head at any moment and that terrifies me."

"It is different this time because God--"

"Joe, this isn't the first time God has shown you your mistakes."

"I know."

"You know but what? You love me? Love is an action and I don't mean the action of you leaving bruises over my body."

"Torre, I know."

"Then what else do you want because I've given you every part of me and each time you break it, bruise it or walk over it. And the saddest part, you have the audacity to expect me to repair the broken pieces of myself by myself."

"Just try."

"I have tried!" She yells. "You were too busy knocking me down to see it. Now, since we *are* being honest, I don't know if I want to try anymore because I don't have any places left for you to scar."

"Can you just believe me, this time?"

"I really want to but I don't."

I stand up. "Will you at least think about it?"

"I have."

I hang my head and walk out because rejection is hard for me to take. And I know if I stay, I'll only get angry and Torre doesn't deserve that when I was the one who asked her to be honest.

I get in my truck and see a missed call and text from Carmen.

HER: Joe, I need to see you.

I lay the phone down without responding. It dings again.

HER: Please come, I need to talk to you about something important.

HER: Joe, please!

ME: Where are you?

HER: Home

ME: I'm on the way.

When I pull up to Carmen's house, she's standing outside. I roll the window down. "What's up?"

"Dang, why the attitude?"

"Look, you called me, remember?"

"Can I at least get in?"

I pop the locks.

She gets in and just sits there.

"Carmen, what do you want, I don't have all day."

"Do you ever think about us?"

"What? No, why would I think about us? We both know how disastrous we were together."

"We were young and dumb then."

"And not meant for each other. Is this what you wanted to talk about? If so, get out."

"Can I taste you?" She blurts.

"Carmen, I have a lot on my mind and I don't feel like playing with you. I thought you really needed something."

"I do, I need you."

I look at her. "I know you didn't call me over her for this shit."

"Why not? You never had a problem with it before. In fact, do you remember how you would come to my house every Sunday, before service, and tune me up for the week?"

"Well, a lot has changed. I've changed and it's been over a year since you and I have been together."

"That's the problem. Come on Joe."

"I thought you were into girls now?"

"I am but you know I can never get enough of you. Please, just a taste." She says reaching over the console to grab me between the legs.

I cannot lie, my soldier instantly stood at attention. Carmen and I were like gas and fire but the sex was always amazing and she gives the best head and hand job.

"I can tell he misses me." She says rubbing him through my pants. "Come on Joe, please?" She pouts.

"No, I am not about to reopen this can of worms. I've done enough already. I can't." I push her hand away. "I need to make my relationship with Torre work so let's just leave well enough alone."

"Come on Joe, you know I will never tell our secrets."

I look around.

"What are you worried about? Your windows are tinted but if you're that scared, pull in the driveway or come inside."

"I'm not going in that house. Where is your dad?"

"Sleeping. Joe, you're wasting time."

I look around, one last time. "Make it fast but this is the last time."

I slide my seat back as far as it goes before unzipping my pants to free my throbbing penis. She smiles before climbing over the console, sliding down, between my legs, under the steering wheel.

She covers him with her mouth making every inch disappear.

"Damn, you've always been good at this." I say pulling her hair back to see her face.

She releases him and licks a trail down to my balls before sucking on each one. She looks up at me and I smile.

"You're still a freak."

"You used to love it." She says before continuing to work. I twist her hair around my hand, in order to watch the juices seep from the corners of her mouth as I push in and out.

"Uh, shit!" I holler out.

She moves and covers my mouth with hers, not waiting for permission to sit on him. I close my eyes when I feel the heat and moistness of her. She remains still as her walls contract around my penis. It's like feeling a heartbeat.

"Damn, you feel good."

"You missed this, didn't you?"

She grabs the back of the seat and begins to ride. I hold her at the waist and she bucks harder and faster.

"Oh shit." She coos into my mouth. "Cum with me daddy."

"Ah fuck!" I groan into her ear. "Don't stop, stay just like that. Yea, like that." I say releasing into her.

We stay there for a second before she kisses me on the lips.

"I knew you missed me. Why don't you come inside and spend the night."

"Carmen, I am not spending the night with you. I have a wife at home. Besides, your dad--"

"I told you he's sleeping."

"I don't care, I am not staying. Now move, I need to get home to my wife."

"When can I see you again?"

"I told you this was the last time."

"You always say that." She says kissing me.

I push her away. "Carmen, stop. This was a mistake and it will never happen again."

She moves to kiss me again.

"STOP! Get the hell out of my truck."

"Fuck you Joe!"

She opens the door and jumps down out the truck. I sit there for a minute before looking down to see the front of my pants are covered with our juices.

I pull my shirt out to cover it up.

"SHIT!" I say hitting the steering wheel.

Daphne

I take my time getting to Torre's house after getting her call. Walking in, I yell her name.

"In the living room." She says.

"What's wrong now?"

"What has Joe done, this time?"

"What are you talking about?"

"He came home with his fake tears and this, God has shown me my mistakes and I'm ready to be a better man, speech." She says mimicking his voice.

I just look at her.

"Torre, did you really call me over her for this crap?"

"I just want to know if I should believe him or if this is another lie."

"Girl, if that Negro is breathing and his mouth is moving, nine times out of ten he's lying. Why are you acting like you've never heard this song? Hell, you made up the dance moves."

"What is that supposed to mean?" She asks.

"Look Torre, I am at my wit's end with you and Joe. You know what he's capable of yet you stay. You know he's a monster because you've seen him in costume but every time he takes it off, you wash it and put it up until he needs it again. You take whatever he dish out, whether you like it or not and now you want to act like this confession is something new. Girl bye, you are not stupid so stop acting like it."

"Wow! I am glad to know how you really feel."

"I'm sorry for it coming out this way but I will not apologize for what I said. I am tired, very tired and unlike you--"

"Unlike me? Daphne, you can stand there and act like you got all your crap together but you are just as much a victim of Joe's crap as I am. The only difference between us, he physically beats me but we both have scars so save your melodramatic speech. You always ask me why I stay but why are you here when you can quit at any time."

"You're right. I can quit but I still have the secrets in my gut and *unlike you*, your scars heal and go away, mine don't."

"Who told you the scars of physical abuse heal and they damn sure don't go away? Just because you cannot see them, doesn't mean they aren't there. Do you not realize the many nights I toss and turn? Or the days I have to walk around, my own home, on egg shells because I don't know who will come through the door. Daphne, you get paid to hide his secrets so you can cut and run at any time. Me, I'm pregnant with a child and I don't know if my husband will snap and kill me before I even feel him or her move."

"Aw," I say. "That was such a moving speech but you're telling it to the wrong person. I am not the one who needs to know this shit Torre, your husband does."

"What good does it do? All it takes is one wrong word to set him off. The next time he calls you, it may be because he's finally killed me."

"I'm sorry I have made you feel that way."

We both turn at the sound of Joe's voice.

"You're not really sorry until you are willing to change." I tell him.

"I am and that's what I told Torre earlier but she doesn't believe me."

"How can I Joe? You're probably coming in, right now, from another women's house."

"That's not true."

"Then where have you been?" Torre asks.

"I just needed to clear my head."

"Oh, which one?" I ask.

He looks at me and I shrug.

"Listen, I've enjoyed this get together but I'm out."

"Daphne wait because there is something I need to tell you and Torre."

"Joe, I don't want to hear whatever it is. Goodbye."

"I'm leaving," he blurts.

I stop and turn around. "Leaving?"

"Yes, I need to get away."

"Are you seriously about to take a vacation?" I ask. "You selfish, low down, penis slinging hypocrite."

"Dee stop, please! I am not taking a vacation."

"Then where are you going?" Torre asks. "Are you leaving the church?"

"Yes but only for a little while because I've messed up and lost control of my life. I need help."

I laugh. "Sound the violin and cue the lights. It's show time people!"

"I am being serious Daphne, I need help!" He yells.

"Daphne and I know that but what has happened to make you finally realize it because I've been begging and pleading with you to get help for five years now."

"Girl, he's had an epiphany. A come to Jesus moment. He's seen the light." I laugh.

"I cannot explain it Torre."

"You need to try because I am not buying what you're selling. Are you in some kind of trouble?"

"No, well yes but not the illegal kind."

"Then what? Did you get somebody pregnant?" Torre asks.

"No, that would be easier to deal with." He says sitting down.

"THEN WHAT? I am tired of playing this game. What have you done now?" I yell.

"I've been unfaithful."

"Boy, that's nothing new." I say. "Everybody knows you got a community penis."

"Daphne, can you please stop with the jokes?"

"Who's joking?"

"Joe, I am going to ask again, why the sudden change of heart? We're being honest, right?" Torre asks.

"I got a letter from the health department."

"Oh that," I say. "It wasn't a big deal earlier."

Torre looks at me before turning back to Joe. "What did it say?"

"For me to call them to discuss an important health matter."

"What does that mean? Are you saying you may have a STD or worse HIV?"

"I DON'T KNOW."

"Wow. It isn't enough for you to put me through hell behind closed doors and embarrass me in the church but you don't even have the common decency to use protection."

"I always use protection, I wouldn't do that to you."

"Oh, I should be grateful but I have a hard time believing that seeing you're a habitual liar."

"And you have every right not to believe me."

"So what now?" I interject.

"I'm leaving."

"Running isn't going to solve this, Joe."

"I'm not running Dee but I am honest enough to know, staying in Memphis will not help me, right now. I need to take some time away and disconnect from everything and everybody."

"What about the church?"

"That's where I'll need you, Dee, to handle everything."

"And what about me? Am I supposed to just stay here while you're out, wherever and doing whoever?"

"It's not like that Torre. I'm going to get help so I can be a better husband and father to that baby you're carrying. All I need is for you to give me another chance."

She walks over to him. "Joe, I love you and I hope you find the peace you need to be a better man but I will not be here when you get back."

Torre

I walk into the bedroom, slam the door and fall onto my knees crying and praying to God.

I get up and walk into the bathroom, turning on the shower. Standing under the warm water I allow, what will be, the final tears to flow. I've made it up in my mind to no longer be a victim.

Once I am done, I stand in front of the mirror, looking at the scars and bruises that are still healing on my body. I don't even recognize the face looking back at me because I'm not the same person I was five years ago.

I am ashamed.

The girl glaring back at me is worn down and battered. She is bruised and barely recognizable.

I yell, with all my power, before taking my brush from the sink and throwing it into the mirror.

"How could you let yourself get here Torre? How?"

I continue to scream until Joe and Daphne run in. When they try to walk toward me, I back up.

"Don't touch me. Get out!"

"Baby--"

"GET OUT!"

I slide down onto the rug, on the bathroom floor naked, crying and surrendering.

I begin speaking to God out loud.

"I'm tired God and I cannot go on like this. Please show me the way because I can no longer do it on my own. This pit is overpowering me and

I can't see how to get out. My body is bruised, my spirit is crushed and my feet are burned from walking over the coals of my circumstance. I am cried out and just need you to free me because I cannot bring this baby into this hell I find myself in. Dear God, I need you. I need you to hear my plea and answer me. I'm tired and in need of restoration. Please God."

After a little while, Daphne comes in with my robe. I don't fight her this time. She covers me with the robe and helps me up. I fall into her arms.

"You're always strong for everybody else Dee but who is there for you?" I ask her.

When I step back, I see something I've never seen before.

Tears.

"Oh Daphne."

"I'm sorry." She says stepping back. "I've got to go."

She runs out, leaving me standing there. I have never, in all the years I've known her, seen her cry.

I lay across the bed, tired from everything.

Sometime later, I open my eyes and my stomach growls. I get up and put on some underwear, a pair of jeans, a t-shirt and flats. I get ready to walk out the room when Joe comes in.

"Hey, I didn't know you were up. Where are you going?"

"Out."

He grabs my arm.

"I asked you a question."

"Is this the new Joe?" I ask looking down at his hand gripping my arm.

He lets me go. "I'm sorry. Will you please tell me where you're going?"

"I'm going to get something to eat."

"Good, I haven't had anything all day. Let's go."

I roll my eyes as he turns to follow me out of the bedroom.

We get to his truck.

"What do you have a taste for?"

"I was--"

"What about the new steak place in Olive Branch?" He asks cutting me off.

"All the way down there?"

"It'll only take about 30 minutes. You don't have anything else to do, do you?"

"I guess not."

Pulling up to the restaurant, Joe parks before coming around to open my door. After speaking to the hostess, she shows us to our table.

"Your server is Anastasia and she'll be right with you."

Joe gets this weird look on his face.

"It's a little drafty at this table, can we move somewhere else? Maybe in the back?"

"Of course."

"Joe?" Someone says while we're getting up.

We both turn to see a young lady, no more than twenty and very pregnant.

He stands in front of me.

"Why haven't you been answering my calls?" She asks.

"Ma'am, I am so sorry. I got your message the other day but I haven't had the opportunity to speak to the board about your request. Why don't you call the church on Monday and I will see what we can do to help you. Now, if you'll excuse me. My wife--"

"Your wife!" She screams. "You said the two of you weren't together anymore but I guess that was another lie. Like the one you told me, saying you were going to be there for me and this baby."

"Joe, who is this?" I ask stepping from behind him.

"Who the fuck are you?" She ask getting loud.

"Baby, she's a young lady who lives in the church community and she's fallen on hard times."

She laughs. "Oh, so that's what we're doing now?"

The hostess steps in front of her but she pushes her out the way.

"Stop lying! Lady, I am not some girl who lives in the community that has fallen on hard time. The only hard thing I've fallen on is his cock! Isn't that right Joe? How else could I be pregnant with your baby?"

"Wow." I laugh. "You lowdown motherf--"

"Torre." He says turning to look at me. "You don't want to do this."

"Me? I'm not the one standing here airing your dirty laundry. Is she lying Joe?"

"Look lady, I don't know who you are but this is between me and Joe." She says walking closer to me.

"Little girl, you don't know me so I suggest you back up."

"Anastasia please!" Joe yells.

She picks up the rolled silverware, from her tray, and slings it at him barely missing his head.

I look around to see people in the restaurant talking and laughing while some are recording on their phone. I shake my head and walk away.

After a few minutes, Joe comes out to where I'm standing outside the restaurant.

"Let's go." He says walking pass me.

When he realizes I am not behind him, he turns around.

"Torre, let's go."

"I'm not going anywhere with you. I've called for an Uber."

He lets out a breath before walking over and snatching me by the arm.

"Please don't make me embarrass you."

"More embarrassed than I already am. People were recording Joe! This shit will be all over social media in a few minutes but again, I'm the one who is wrong."

"Can we talk about this at home?"

"I am not going with you."

"You don't have a choice." He says pulling me toward the truck.

He pushes me in and slams the door before getting into the driver's seat. He starts the truck and as we pull out, I see Anastasia waddling out of the restaurant screaming at his truck.

"Just give me another chance Torre. I'm changing Torre. I messed up Torre. I'll never hurt you again Torre." I say mimicking his voice. "I asked you if you've gotten anybody pregnant and you lied. You looked me in my face and proudly lied without an ounce of respect for me. I shouldn't be surprised but she's barely an adult, Joe! You're having a baby with a child."

"She's not a child."

"Is that all you want to correct?"

"I don't know if it is my baby."

"But it's a possibility?"

He doesn't answer.

"You low down, good for nothing, rotten to the core motherfucker." I say slowly to pronounce every letter.

"I know you're upset but you better watch your mouth."

"Or what Joe? Huh? For the millionth time, I am made to look like a fool. Oh but this time it was in a restaurant full of people who were laughing and recording. And you say watch my mouth, you should have watched yours!"

He grips the steering wheel.

"Why do I deserve this? What have I done to deserve any of this?"

He doesn't say anything.

"Answer me! You at least owe me that."

"I don't owe you shit." He says back handing me. "I told you to watch your mouth. This is why you are always getting your ass beat. You don't know when to shut up."

I wipe my mouth.

"I know I fucked up and I don't need you to keep reminding me. Do me a favor and shut up."

"Thank you Joe."

"What?" He says.

"Thank you."

"For what?"

"For giving me a way out." I say before grabbing the steering wheel.

"Torre, stop! Let go of the wheel. You're going to make us--"

Daphne

I am sitting at the bar, in the Hilton Hotel, nursing my third glass of wine, which is now warm; replaying the last few weeks in my mind.

"Is this seat taken?"

"No," I say removing my purse from the chair but never looking up.

"You look nice tonight, are you here by yourself?" She asks me.

I look up to ask to be left alone but then I see her and nod.

"I'm sorry. If you want to be left alone--"

"No, you're fine. Have a seat."

"Can I get you another glass of wine?" She asks motioning for the bartender to bring her a glass.

"No thanks, this is my third one. I like to remember what I get into."

"Is that right? And what do you like to get into?"

"Anything good and satisfying to my desires." I say playing with the rim of the glass.

"Are you married?"

"No, you?"

"Happily divorced. I'm Carmen, by the way."

"It is nice to meet you Carmen. I'm Daphne."

"What brings you out on this Friday night Daphne?"

"Clearing my mind. What about you?"

"Same."

There is silence as she sips from her glass.

"I hope this doesn't offend you but are you into women?"

I nod.

"What about you?"

"I like men and women." She says. "Look, I'm a straight forward person who doesn't like to beat around the bush, unless it's between the legs of a sexy ass woman. It's been a minute since I've had the pleasure of a woman and seeing you in that dress, with those legs are driving me crazy."

I slowly uncross my legs turning to her.

"Is this the kind of thing you do, pick up women in bars? I could be a serial killer for all you know."

"No, this is my first time and I would hope you aren't but if you are, can you give me an orgasm first."

I laugh.

"If you are interested and willing to take a risk, follow me." She says downing the rest of her wine and throwing a twenty dollar bill on the bar.

I am skeptical of what exactly this means but I follow anyway. We get to the elevators and as one opens she pulls me inside covering my mouth, playfully sucking my tongue. When the elevator dings, we are at the entrance door for the roof.

"Are we supposed to be up here?"

"Are you scared?"

"No but--"

"Then come on."

I slip off my shoes and follow. When she finally gets the door open, we walk out on the roof and the view is beautiful. I sit my shoes and bag beside the wall and lean over a little.

"This view is amazing."

Carmen comes up behind me, lifting my dress.

"Yes it is." She says kissing on my butt. "Daphne, you're a bad girl." Referring to me having on no panties.

When she rubs between my legs, she moans and I am sure she's thanking the fresh Brazilian wax I got a few days ago.

She doesn't hesitate in spreading my legs and inserting a finger into my moistness causing me to bend over, a little more.

"Mmm."

"You like that?"

"Yes," I moan turning around to give her full view of my lady.

"Damn, you smell good. Can I taste you baby?"

"Help yourself, she's yours tonight."

She smiles before my vagina is covered with wet, warm lips causing me to moan out. I grab the back of her head as I enjoy the feel of her tongue. After a few minutes, I pull her up and begin to lick my juices from her face.

Her hand finds its way back down and I start to gyrate on her fingers. She doesn't break our contact as I moan into her mouth from the orgasm moving through me.

She pushes deeper. "Give me all that, yeah, just like that."

I am holding on to her as she smacks my lady like she's making sure to get every drop.

When she steps back, I grab her hand, leading her to this power box thing. She removes her panties before climbing on it. I spread her legs, running my hands down the inside of her thighs, licking my lips before using my tongue to form circles on her clit.

"Yea," she moans as I spread her lips and suck her clit into my mouth. Flicking it around with my tongue, she grabs the back of my head.

"Shit!" She screams. "I'm cumming!"

I don't release her or stop, instead I suck harder.

She is moaning and cursing so loud that we do not hear the door open.

"Hey, what are y'all doing?"

I raise up and kiss her in the mouth before turning to him.

"Sorry officer, I was just enjoying dessert."

"Uh," he swallows. Y'all are not supposed to be up here."

"We're leaving officer or you can join us."
She says to him before sucking on my ear.

He doesn't move or say anything so I turn
back to her, inserting two fingers into her
opening. She is sucking on my tongue as I move
my fingers like I'm telling her to come to me.

"Oh God." She screams.

I move, a little, to the side to give him full
view and also because I know she's about to
squirt.

"O–H–S–H–I–T!"

"Damn." He says walking towards us but
someone says something on his radio.

"Y'all got to go but can I get your number?"

Carmen takes her panties and stuff them
into his mouth before grabbing my hand. I stop
and grab my shoes and purse. By the time we

make it back to the elevator, we are both laughing.

"Oh my God, I have never done anything like that."

"Daphne, that was amazing."

When we make it downstairs to the lobby, she kisses me on the lips.

"Can we exchange numbers?" She asks.

"I'd like that."

After putting her number in my phone and me calling her from mine, she kisses me one last time before walking off. I walk into the bathroom to freshen up. Getting ready to pull the door open, I stop when my phone vibrates with a call from Torre's mom, which is odd.

"Ms. Banks, is everything okay? Oh my God. Where? Okay. I'm on the way."

Twenty minutes later, I rush into Regional One.

"May I help you?"

"Yes, I am looking for a patient."

"Name?"

"Torre, T–o–r–r–e, Thornton."

"Are you family?"

"Yes, I'm her sister."

"One minute. Mrs. Thornton is in the critical bay. If you take this hall, down to the double doors and press the button on the wall to be buzzed in. Go to that nurse's station and they can help you from there."

Power walking through the double doors, I turn the corner to see Torre's mom pacing.

"Ms. Banks."

"Oh Daphne." She cries.

"What happened? Is Torre okay?"

"She was in a car accident."

"Has anyone talked to you?"

"No, not since I got here."

I lead her to some chairs and sit her down.

"Stay here and I'll see what I can find out."

I walk to the nurse's station and she lets me know a doctor should be out soon to talk to us.

I go back and let Ms. Banks know.

"Do you know what happened?"

"No, I don't know anything. A police officer showed up at my house and said they'd been involved in an accident and bought me here."

"They?"

"Yes, she was in the truck with Joe. I can't lose my baby." She cries.

"They will be okay." I tell her. "They have to be."

We've been sitting in the waiting room for over an hour when two doctors finally come out.

"Thornton family."

"Right here." I say jumping up from my seat.

"You're with the family of Carmen and Joseph Thornton?"

"Yes, we both are."

"My name is Dr. Pelissero and I am looking after Mr. Thornton. He is in critical condition because he sustained some internal damage that is causing blood to pool in his abdomen. We cannot be sure of where the blood is coming from or the full extent of his injuries until we open him up. He will be taken into surgery in the next hour.

He also has a broken leg, which will also be repaired during surgery."

"What about my daughter?"

"My name is Dr. Hartville and your daughter sustained some injuries but we don't believe them to be life threatening. She hit her head and although she hasn't regained consciousness, a CAT scan has ruled out bleeding or swelling. There are no internal injuries but her left wrist is broken which will require surgery."

"When will she wake up?"

"Right now we don't know but we will continue to monitor her for signs of late onset head trauma and wait for her to wake up on her own."

"My God." Ms. Banks cry.

"What about the baby?" I ask.

"Baby?" Her mom exclaims. "Torre is pregnant?"

"Yes, she looks to be about twelve weeks but the baby is fine, for now."

"Can we see them?"

"You can see Mrs. Thornton now and Mr. Thornton once he is in recovery. Follow me."

Torre

Four days later

I blink my eyes which feels like they weigh a ton. I try to move but it causes pain to shoot through my body. I blink again to get my eyes to focus but then, I hear my momma praying.

"God, your blood still works. Your blood can heal. Your blood can deliver. It's been four days now God, I need you to work and bring my baby back to me. Work now God, you have too because I can't lose her."

I feel the tears burning the sides of my face.

"Momma," I whisper raising my hand. "Momma."

"Oh my Jesus, Torre." She says moving to take my hand. "Baby, say my name again. Please."

"Momma."

"Oh God! Can you open your eyes?"

"It hurts."

"I know but try for momma. Please baby."

I blink a few times and they finally open. I see momma's face but it's blurry.

"There she is. I am so happy to see those beautiful eyes."

"Momma, what happened?"

"Shh, we can talk later. Let me get the doctor." She presses the button on the side of the bed.

"Can I help you?"

I cringe from the loudness of the nurse's voice.

"Yes, can you let the doctor know that my daughter is awake?"

"Yes ma'am, he will be right in."

Ten minutes later, the door opens and the doctor comes in followed by two nurses.

"Mrs. Thornton, my name is Dr. Hartville, can you hear me?" He says shining a light into my eyes.

I squeeze my eyes shut and shake my head yes.

"I know the light hurts but I need you to open your eyes. Do you know where you are?"

I shake my head no.

"You're in the hospital. You were in a serious accident with your husband. Do you remember that?"

"Joe," is the only word I could say before my eyes start to close again.

"Stay with me." He says.

I open my eyes again.

"Can you squeeze my hands?"

I do but I can't keep my eyes open.

"Can you feel this?" He asks rubbing something cold on my feet which causes me to jump.

He turns to my mom and I hear him saying, "Now that she's awake, we will do another CAT scan just to make sure there's nothing major going on. Her body has been through an ordeal but she will be okay."

"Oh thank God."

"Mrs. Thornton, are you in any pain?"

"All over," I whisper.

"I'll have the nurse give you something. We will do another CAT scan but I don't foresee it being different that the previous one. You had surgery, yesterday, to repair some broken bones in your left wrist which means you will be in a cast for up to six weeks. Do you have any questions for me?"

"My baby?"

"We performed an ultrasound when you were brought in and your baby is fine. I will send an OB by to check on you and I'll come back later."

When the doctor leaves, mom comes back over to the bed and kisses me on the forehead.

"I'm sorry momma."

"It's not your fault, you were in an accident."

"I caused the accident."

"What? Why would you cause an accident?"

"Where's Joe?"

"He's down the hall."

"Is he okay?"

"He will be. Daphne is with him. Now, what did you mean?"

I moan from the pain. I don't know if it's coming from my heart or my body but it hurts and I start to cry.

"I'm sorry momma. I should have told you everything."

"Shh," she says before she begins to pray again. "Dear God, thank you for hearing my prayer. Thank you for saving my daughter and grandbaby. I know I've asked a lot of you lately but I need you, one more time. You're healing the physical, now I need you to heal the mental. God whatever it is Torre is battling with, repair it. Whatever demons she'd had to fight, I ask you to take over. God, we are tapping you in because she can no longer fight it alone. Show up Father and let her know you've never left her. Be her guide, now God, so that she may find peace in this weary land. I pray in your son Jesus name, Amen."

Joseph

I open my eyes and begin to panic when I don't recognize where I am.

"Joe, calm down. Joe, its Dee, please calm down."

When she looks at me and smile I stop fighting.

"Where am I?"

"You're in the hospital. Stay calm and I will get the doctor." She says. "Do you understand?"

I nod my head yes.

She leaves and I close my eyes only to open them when I hear the door open, a few minutes later.

"Mr. Thornton, my name is Dr. Pelissero. You're in the hospital. Can you tell me your first name?"

"Joseph."

"Okay Joseph, I'm going to examine you now." He says.

"OH," I groan from the pain in my stomach. "What happened?"

"You were in an accident."

I look confused.

"Where's Torre?"

"She's fine Joe." Daphne says.

"Did she leave me?"

"She should but no, she's down the hall recovering. She was in the accident with you."

I close my eyes again.

"Mr. Thornton, you suffered some internal damage to your spleen. We removed it during surgery as well as repaired the injury to your leg.

A rod had to be placed in it, so it will be a while before you'll be able to fully walk again, without aid. Do you understand?"

I nod.

He removes the bandage from my stomach. "You are healing perfectly fine. The nurse will change your bandages and the staples we used to close you up will need to be removed in about two weeks."

"Are there any long term complications?" Daphne asks.

"When removing the spleen, he can run the risk of getting infections because the spleen plays a crucial role in the body's ability to fight them off. However, we will monitor him, while he's here and once he's discharged, he will need to be careful when he gets a common cold or infection; making sure he sees his primary doctor as soon as possible for antibiotics."

"Thank you doctor." She says.

"No problem. Do you have any other questions?"

"Yes." Joe says. "Did you test my blood?"

"Of course. Why do you ask?"

I look at Daphne.

"Before the accident, he received a letter from the health department. We are not sure the exact reasoning behind it but did you all test him for any STDs and HIV?"

He touches the IPad in his hands. "We tested you for HIV and it was negative. We also ran bloodwork for signs of infection and there were clean as well. I would recommend seeing your primary care as soon as you can to have him or her re-run any test you need."

"Thank you doctor."

.

"Can I see my wife?" I ask.

"I will talk to your wife's doctor and see if that's possible. In the meantime, try to get some rest and I will be back in the morning to check on you."

He walks out leaving the nurse behind. She walks over with items to change his bandage.

"Mr. Thornton, I'm going to redress your wound. It shouldn't hurt but if it does, please let me know."

She raises his gown and I can see her eyes drifting pass his stomach. When she looks back at him, he smiles at her and I shake my head.

She is taking her time, rubbing on his stomach and he is eating it up.

"Um, are you done?" I ask.

"Yes, I am." She says. "I'll be back later sir."

"You still haven't gotten enough?" I tell him.

"What happened to me?"

"How in the hell should I know?"

"The last thing I remember is going out to eat--" I stop when the memories begin flooding back.

"What?" She asks.

"This is my fault."

"That's not shocking. What did you do?"

"I took Torre to a new restaurant in Olive Branch for dinner."

"And?"

"Anastasia worked there."

"Anastasia? Anastasi--wait, isn't she the young girl who came to the church for help?"

"Yes."

"What does she have to do with this?"

I don't answer.

"Please don't tell me you've been sleeping with that girl. She's what, 19?"

"21."

"Got damn it Joe! Did she cause a scene?"

"A big one and she's pregnant."

"OH.MY.GOD!"

Just then someone knocks on the door.

"Come in."

In walks Deacon Harper and Thorpe.

"Good afternoon." Thorpe says. "It's good to see you in the land of the living."

"Deacons, what brings you by?"

"Well, we were wondering if you've seen this."

He press play and holds up his phone with a video of me, Torre and Anastasia in the restaurant.

After having to listen to the deacons rant and rave, Daphne finally walks them out. I am mentally preparing myself for when she returns.

"A child Joe? That girl is only a child." She says before the door even closes.

"I messed up."

"No boo, you fucked up!"

"Is Torre okay?" I ask.

"Barely but Joe, when does this stop? Haven't you done enough?"

Before I can answer, Carmen comes busting through the door.

"Oh my God Joe, are you okay?" She asks running to my bed.

I cry out in pain when she falls over me.

"I'm sorry, did I hurt you?"

When she looks up and sees me, her eyes get big. "Daphne?"

"Carmen? What are you doing here?"

"I was about to ask you the same thing."

I'm looking from one to the other. "You two know each other?"

"You can say that." Carmen says.

"How do you know Joe?" Daphne asks.

"He's my ex-husband."

Daphne

I walk down the hall to Torre's room, in a state of shock. I tap on the door before opening it.

"Daphne, come in."

"Hey girl, how are you feeling?"

"I will be much better once I can get out of here."

"Where is your mom?"

"She went to the cafeteria. Can I ask you a favor?"

"Anything."

"Will you take her home so she can get some rest? She's been here for almost a week."

"Of course. What else do you need?"

"A good divorce attorney."

I grab her hand.

"Did you know Dee?"

I drop my head.

"Dee, did you know about that girl?"

I sigh. "Yes, I know of her because she came to the church about a year ago to ask for help but she never showed up for the deacon's meeting so I assumed she didn't need it anymore. But I promise you, I did not know he was sleeping with her. I only found out a little while ago, from Deacon Thorpe who has the video from the restaurant."

"She's just a child." She says above a whisper. "And she's pregnant."

"I know."

"What is wrong with him?"

"He is suffering from a disease." I say.

"What? Is that why he got the letter from the Health Department."

"Oh no, the doctors say he is clean from all that. The disease I'm talking about is called Power and if he doesn't get the help he needs, soon, it's going to kill him."

Ms. Banks walks in.

"Oh Daphne, I didn't know you were here."

"Yes ma'am." I say getting up to give her a hug. "How are you?"

"You don't have to worry about me, I'm fine. I'm just glad my baby is getting well. How is Joe?" She asks.

"He's alive. The doctor says they will keep him here a few days to make sure he doesn't set up an infection and then he can go home. What about you?" I ask turning back to Torre. "What did the doctor say?"

"I have to wear this cast for about six weeks but other than that, I'm good."

"What about the little one?"

"So far so good. An OB came by and we heard the heartbeat. When I get out of here, I'm going to find a good OBGYN just to make sure."

"I see a doctor out in Cordova who is a really great one. Her name is Dr. Meade. If you want, I can give you her number."

"That will be great."

Before her mom gets comfortable, I stop her.

"Mom, I asked Dee to take you home to get some rest."

"I'm not leaving you."

"It will make me feel better if you would go and get some rest and hopefully by the time you come back in the morning, I will be going home."

"Are you sure?"

"Yes ma'am. I am sure."

"Let me stop in Joe's room and then I'll meet you at the elevators." I tell Ms. Banks.

I leave out and walk the few doors down to Joe's room. I knock and slowly open the door.

"Is your guest gone?"

"Yea. How is Torre?"

"So we're not going to talk about the fact you have a whole ex-wife?"

"No."

"Figures."

"How's Torre."

"Why do you care? I mean, if she meant anything to you, neither of you would be here."

"Dee, please. I am not in the mood for this right now. Is she alright?"

"Hell no but she will be. Now, do you need anything because I'm about to leave to take Ms. Banks home."

"Dee, I really messed up."

"I know."

"I need help."

"I know that too."

"I am the pastor of a large and growing church here in Memphis and I don't even respect the sanctity of God. I can put together a well formatted sermon and I can whoop with the best preachers in the city but at the end of the day, what good am I doing? I allowed the comfortability of power to consume me Dee. I let the attention and the platform take me away from what God has called me to do. And now, I am about to lose it all, including my wife. And for what?"

"Wow," I say clapping. "That was, that was bullshit and we both know it."

"I don't expect you to understand."

"Oh, I understand, I just don't believe you. You forget, we've danced to this song too many times and the moves are all the same. So forgive me, Pastor, if I can't take your word for it. Anyway, I'll be back later on. Your phone was in your pants pocket at the time of the accident. The screen is a little cracked but it's useable. I laid it on the table, right there. If you need me, use it."

Torre

I am watching the sunset from my window when I hear the door open. I don't turn my head, thinking it's just the nurse coming to check my vitals.

"Torre."

I close my eyes and let out a sigh. "What do you want Joe?"

I turn over to see a nurse wheeling him in.

"Thank you." He says to her.

"Press the call button when you're ready to go back to your room." She says walking out.

"Torre baby, I am so sorry."

"Sorry you got caught, again?"

"No, sorry for everything. All of this is because of me but the doctor says I don't have any diseases."

"So what do you want? A congratulations or do you expect me to say I forgive you this time? Maybe you're waiting to hear me say we can go back home as the loving pastor and first lady and make this right? That we can fix this? Well, there is no more fixing Joseph Thornton. This is your bed of thorns to lie in and from now on you will do so by yourself."

"You didn't have to try and kill me to get your point across." He smiles.

"You deserved it and nothing about any of this is funny."

He tries to grab my hand but I snatch it back.

"Why wasn't I enough?"

He sighs. "The truth?"

"If you can even tell the truth."

"Truth is, you were enough for my spirit but not my flesh."

I chuckle. "Got it."

"When the doors of Assembly opened and the congregation started to grow, so did my ego. I had women throwing themselves at me and it made me feel good. The power that came with being on such a big platform went to my head."

"Which one?"

"Both."

"Finally, the truth!"

"Torre, I knew what I was doing but I thought I was in control. Every time I did something I knew I shouldn't, I thought I could handle it. Until I couldn't. Things started happening too fast and before I knew it, the plank of power I was standing on, gave way and I found myself drowning."

"Joe, all of this sounds good but when someone is standing on a plank, they wear a lifejacket and when they are drowning, they damn sure ask for help."

"I am asking for help."

"We both know it's only because you got caught. Can I ask you a question?"

"Anything."

"Why the abuse?"

"Control. Plain and simple. I was losing the control over what was happening to me and the one thing I could control was you."

"But I was already submissive to you because my mother showed me how to be a good wife. And I was a damn good one. I was your Proverbs 31 wife, standing next to you even though I heard other woman whispering about you. I was the one praying for you even on the nights you didn't come home and I knew where you were. I was the one who cooked even though you barely ate a lot of the meals. I was the one who loved every part of you, even those that are dirty and you still treated me like trash. Yet, every time I got up and washed the stench away because I was First Lady."

I wipe the tears falling. "Each time you hit me, I stood under the water washing away the blood before covering the bruises with makeup and clothes because church folk said, stay in your marriage. It was my prayers that hid your faults. It was my prayers that covered you. It was my prayers that kept Assembly of God. And each time you looked at me, you never gave a damn."

"I'm sorry."

"No Joe, this time you don't get to apologize. This time, I'm the one who's sorry for staying with a piece of man like you. I'm the one who is sorry for giving my all to you when I knew it was too much for you to handle. I'm the one who is sorry for ever thinking my favor was fashioned for you. This time, I'm the one who is sorry for ever giving you a position you weren't trained for."

"Torre–"

I push the call button.

"How can I help you?"

"Mr. Thornton is ready to go back to his room now."

"A nurse will be right in."

"This time, I am taking the broken pieces and putting them in the hands of somebody who can repair them and it's not you. Goodbye Joe."

The next morning, I sign the release papers and pack up the few things I have here, at the hospital, while momma waits to take me home.

"You ready?" She asks.

"Definitely."

"Are you going home?"

"If you mean your home, yes but I do need to go by the house?"

"Sure baby, what do you need to get?"

"My car and a few things I will need until I can find a new place to live."

"Are you sure about this?"

"Yes ma'am, it's long overdue."

We get to the house and I am finding, with one arm, this to be harder than I expected but mom and I manage the best we can.

After putting the last bag in the trunk, I send momma on, telling her I'll meet her once I lock the house up.

My car is in the driveway, so I let the garage down. Doing one final sweep to make sure I have all my essential things, I open the front door...

"Where's Joe?" She asks pushing her way in.

"Excuse you? How do you know where I live?"

"You aren't the only one who has enjoyed this house." She says smiling.

"You've been in my house?"

"A few times. Anyway, where is Joe?"

"Look little girl--"

"My name is Anastasia."

"Ana--, you know what, I don't care what your name is but you need to get the hell out of my house."

"Lady, I am not here to cause trouble, I just want Joe."

"How old are you?"

"Twenty-one."

"Why are you fooling with someone old enough to be your dad?"

"Not that it is any of your business but I love him and he loves me."

"Joe doesn't know the meaning of love."

"I'm sorry you had to find out about us like that, he was supposed to tell you."

"Tell me what?"

"We're getting married."

"He's already married."

She shrugs. "Not for long because he loves me and our baby and he's going to marry me. Then I can move in here for good."

"Baby, Joe isn't marriage material. Trust me, I've had to learn the hard way."

"You don't know him like I do. All he needs is someone to take care of him. I can do that."

"What can you possibly know about taking care of a grown man? Especially one like Joe. He is a monster, one I hope you've never had the privilege of meeting. If you want some advice--"

"I don't want your advice. Joe says you're crazy and wouldn't leave him alone but now that you know about us, you can go. Besides, I'll never turn my back on him because my son deserves to know his father and I deserve all this." She says waving her arms.

"Wow." I shake my head. "Baby, I hope you will take my advice and run but if you want Joe and his problems, have at it. He's at Regional One, downtown. Good luck to you."

I open the door, let her out before setting the alarm, walking out and locking the door.

Joseph

"Are you ready to go home?" Dee ask walking into my room.

"Yes. Oh, Deacon Harper called this morning and I ask him to meet me at the house."

"When?"

"Now."

"Why?" She asks.

"There are some things I need to discuss with him about me taking some time off."

She doesn't say anything.

"Are you going to say something?"

"There is nothing to say Joe. You need to take some time off."

"What about Torre?" I ask Dee.

"What about her?"

"Is she still here?"

"No, she was released yesterday."

"You're all set Mr. Thornton. Ma'am, you can meet us downstairs at the discharge entrance." The nurse says walking in.

She waits until Dee leaves.

"Are you ready sir?"

"Very." I smile taking her hand. "Thank you for taking such good care of me. You're really good with your hands."

"You think so?" She asks closing the door.

"What are you doing?"

"Checking your bandage one last time."

"No, it's good because the other nurse already changed it." I tell her moving her hand.

"You sure? It looks like it needs addressing." She says kneeling in front of me to rub my erection that's starting to show through my sweatpants. "It will not take long."

She reaches in and pulls out my penis, taking the head into her mouth.

"We really shouldn't—aw!"

She stands up, a little, and begins sucking and rubbing harder and faster. I am gripping the handles of the wheel chair while this girl puts in work. She doesn't stop until I release down her throat.

Standing up, she puts my semi-hard penis back in my pants and wipes her mouth. "If you need a home nurse, call me. I put my number in your phone under Gracie and I left some pictures for you too."

I can't even say anything as she opens the door and pushes me down the hall.

Finally getting home, Dee helps me get settled on the couch in the living room.

Before I have a chance to talk to her, about my plans to leave Memphis for a while, the doorbell rings.

"That's probably Deacon Harper."

When she opens the door, Anastasia burst in.

"Baby, what happened to you? You had me so worried." She asks kneeling at the couch.

"What are you doing here?"

"You haven't been returning my calls and I am not leaving until you talk to me. I went to the hospital and they said you'd been sent home."

"How did you know I was in the hospital?"

"Your wife told me when I came by here yesterday."

"You saw Torre?"

"Yea--"

"Is now a bad time?" Deacon Harper says walking in.

I silently curse under my breath. "Harper, can you give me a minute and I'll be right with you?" I ask nodding at Dee who shows him to the kitchen.

I try to sit up as best I can. "Look Tasia, I know I haven't returned your calls and I will but right now is not a good time."

"It's never a good time with you." She says raising her voice.

I grab her by the chin. "What have I told you about raising your voice to me?"

"I'm sorry daddy, I am just worried about you."

"Thank you but I am about to have a very important meeting with one of my deacons and you cannot be here."

"I can wait in the bedroom for you."

"No! Look, give me an hour and then come back. We will talk then."

"You promise?"

"Yes, now leave."

When she closes the door, Dee comes in.

"Are you ready now or should I wait a few more minutes to see if anymore strays show up?"

"Bring Harper in so I can get this over with."

"Don't get mad at me, daddy." She laughs walking off.

She shows Deacon Harper back in.

"I apologize for that."

"Pastor, what is going on?"

"I'm going to take some time off because I've done some things I am not proud of and before I step back in the pulpit, I need to make myself right before God."

"Does this have anything to do with the video?"

"It's part of it. Look, I don't want to go into details but I need to know I have your support. Thorpe will do whatever he can to turn the members against me while I am away, if he hasn't already."

"Of course you have my support because at the end of the day, you are a man who has faults. Although you are held to a higher standard, it does not exempt you from falling short."

"I appreciate that."

"With that being said, you need to get your shit together. The video, the accusations and now you have a young lady who is pregnant with your child; it is beginning to be too much. The only reason I am willing to stand beside you is because you have too many people depending on you and right now, most of them don't know this side of you. Keep it that way."

"I definitely will."

"While you're out, what do you want me to do?"

"Daphne and I will come up with a list of speakers who can handle the weeks I'll be out. She will be the main contact and she'll also have signing privileges for anything that needs to be handled until I return. For you, I trust you to run things as I would."

"How long will you be out and do you have plans to address the congregation?"

"I'm thinking six to eight weeks. And I haven't thought about how to address them yet."

"Why not do a video that can be played during service." Dee says. "I can record it."

"That's a great idea." Harper adds.

"Do you really think that will work?"

"It can't hurt." He says. "What about your wife?"

"She's staying with her mom. I don't know if she'll be returning to the church but I am going to do whatever I can to repair my marriage."

"Good luck to you sir." Harper stands extending his hand. "Dee, will you send me the video once you're done?"

"I sure will."

Daphne

I show Deacon Harper out before helping Joe to the bathroom to freshen up. I am fixing the pillows on the couch when the doorbell rings.

"Carmen, what are you doing here?"

"Dee, can we talk?"

I step back to let her in, taking her into the kitchen.

"How did you know I'd be here?"

"I just assumed when I went to the hospital and they said Joe had been discharged."

"Um, ok. What did you want to talk about?"

"I had no idea you knew my ex-husband."

"And I had no idea Joe has an ex-wife."

"Yea, he doesn't like to talk about it. We were young when we got married and both stupid and neither of us knew how to be married or faithful. We tried to make it work but after Joe was called to pastor, I knew it was time for me to bail out."

"And you all kept in touch?"

"For the benefits." She smiles.

"So, you two are still sleeping together?"

"We used to. Joe and I were terrible as husband and wife but the sex was always amazing and from time to time, I like the feel of a penis. His penis."

"Wow." I say.

"Anyway, if I had known the two of you were together--"

"Wait, no, it is not like that. I work for Joe as his administrative assistant."

"Oh! You're the Dee he was always talking about? You're his Olivia Pope."

"Unfortunately."

"Look Daphne, I know this may be weird, seeing we just met but I would like to get to know you better." She says walking close to me.

"I don't know Carmen. This is crazy. What am I supposed to tell his wife? Wait, does she even know about you?"

She shrugs. "Joe's wife is not my problem. Now, what do you say? Can we get to know each other? Say yes, you know you want too."

Her hands slide down between my legs.

"Can we?"

"Yes." I moan.

"Good, I'll call you later." She covers my mouth with hers until I hear Joe call my name.

She kisses me one last time before walking out. I turn down the hall to see Joe struggling with the crutches.

"Why didn't you wait for me to help you?"

"You were preoccupied."

I stand behind him as he wobbles over the couch.

"So, you and Carmen, huh?"

"Uh, you and Carmen, huh?" She responds.

"It's not what you think."

"Whatever Joe. Have you thought about what you're going to say?"

"I'm going to let the Lord lead me."

"Finally?"

"Whatever Dee, just get your phone and let's get this over with."

I prop him up on the couch before I sit across from him.

I press play and motion for him to begin.

"Good morning Assembly of God. As most of you, probably know by now, Torre and I were involved in a car accident about a week ago. We are both healing and we would like to thank all of you for your prayers. However, there is another matter I'd like to address. There is a video circulating that I am not proud of. I made a huge mistake which has caused embarrassment to myself, my family and to you. Due to this, I have decided to take some time away from the pulpit. Some of the things you may hear are true and some are not, either way, I am ashamed of the way I have carried myself as your pastor and leader. Please forgive me. Now, in order to truly begin to heal and repair what I've broken, I need to take some time to get myself together. Starting today, I will be taking a six month sabbatical to fast and pray as I consult God for the future direction of my life, family and church. I ask, during this time, that you continue to support Assembly of God and Lady Torre as it is just as hard on her. Be there for one another and as always, pray for your pastor. God bless each of you."

I end the video.

"How was that?" He asks.

"It was honest, something I didn't think was in you."

"I'm trying Dee." I tell her when I hear my phone vibrate on the table. "Can you hand me that?"

"Are you freaking kidding me?"

She turns the phone to show me a nude photo.

"Gracie says hi." She says before throwing the phone at me.

"It's not what you think."

"Who are you fooling? All of this is a joke to you. I ought to delete this video."

"Please don't. I promise it's not what it looks like but this is another reason why I've got to leave as soon as the doctor gives me the clearance."

"I hope he calls tonight."

She leaves out and I pick up the phone.

Anastasia

I wait in my car, in front of his house until I see the man leave. I look at my watch and wait another thirty minutes before getting out and going back to the door.

Before I can ring the doorbell, someone snatches it open.

"You again." She says.

"Who are you?"

"Who is it Dee?" I hear Joe ask.

"Oh, you're Dee. It's nice to meet you, I'm Anastasia."

"I know who you are, what do you want?"

"None of your business. Where is Joe?" I push pass her.

When he sees me, he rolls his eyes.

"Joe, why are treating me like this? You said to come back in an hour. What have I done to you?"

"Anastasia, I am really not in the mood right now."

"And you think I am? I am almost seven months pregnant with YOUR child and you're treating me like some hoe! Look Joe, all I want is for you to acknowledge me and your baby. You were the one who said we would get married. You made all those promises, not me!"

"You are right. I did make you a lot of promises but you should have known none of those were true. I am already married and I love my wife."

"WHAT ABOUT ME?"

"You're a child, for God's sake."

"A child whose virginity you took and now I'm just supposed to walk away while you live happily ever after?"

"I'm sorry but I don't know what else you want from me.

"That's it? You're sorry? What about me? What am I supposed to do with a baby on my own?"

"Stop acting like you are innocent in all of this. You knew exactly what you were getting every time you turned your ass around and backed it up for me to screw. Every time you called me, you knew who I was and what I had to offer. Did I make promises? Yes, but who doesn't when you're in the midst of fornicating. Like I said, I am sorry but you trying to trap me with this baby doesn't change how I feel. You chose to keep it, you raise it."

I wipe the tears. "So, I don't get a say in any of this? I just have to take what you say and go away like a good little puppy?"

He doesn't say anything.

"SAY SOMETHING!"

"Tasia, what do you want me to say? You didn't honestly expect to be my First Lady, did you?" He laughs. "You can't even finish college."

"FUCK YOU JOE! You're a low down dog who will get what's coming to you."

"Is that a threat?" He asks me.

"No, it's a promise and I hope you rot in hell."

He laughs.

"I am glad you think this is funny but it's not. I didn't ask for any of this. You came on to me! You got me pregnant."

"Yea but you didn't stop me."

"All I need is some help." I cry. "This is your baby too which means we have to have some kind of relationship."

"No we don't."

"Can you at least give me money so I can find a better place to live?"

"I'll get Dee to see what she can do and call you. Now, get out of my house and don't ever come here again."

"You are disgusting and I hope you get what's coming to you because you can't keep hurting people and getting away with it."

"Have a great day Anastasia."

I walk out and slam the door. Getting back to my car, I grab my cell phone and dial a number.

"Hey, it's me. I need your help to take care of something."

Torre

It's been two weeks since I moved back with my mom. Standing in the mirror, I turn to the side to rub my baby bump.

"It's just you and me little one but we will make the best of it. And mommy promises to always protect you."

I walk into the kitchen to find momma sitting at the table humming and crying.

"Mom, are you okay."

"Yes baby, I'm okay."

"Why are you crying?"

"It happens sometimes when I'm praying."

I sit next to her and take her hand.

"Torre, how long has Joe been abusing you?"

I drop my head.

She raises it with her hand. "The only time you drop your head is when you are praying. A down head is a sign of defeat and as long as God is your savior, you will never be defeated. Now, how long has this been going on?"

"For the last few years."

"Oh baby. Why didn't you tell me when he first started hitting you?"

"It didn't start off physical. He would yell, throw things and belittle me but I chalked it up to the stress of starting the church. It only got worse as time went on and by time I realized I was in an abusive relationship, it was too late."

"You should have told me."

"It would not have made a difference, momma because I wasn't ready to leave him and telling you would have put a strain on our relationship. I could not let that happen. Plus, I didn't want you worrying about me every time I left going home."

"To be honest, I saw the signs."

"You did?"

"Torre, you're my only daughter which means I can tell when you are not yourself."

"Why didn't you say anything?"

"It wasn't my place for the exact reason you said. You were the one sleeping under his roof and I didn't want to make it harder, for you, by butting in your business. I knew when you were ready for me to know, you'd tell me. Besides, God told me He'd protect you." She says squeezing my hand. "Have you decided what you are going to do?"

"From now on I am putting me first because I have this one to protect." I say rubbing my stomach.

"Have you heard from Joe?"

"Yea, he called a few days ago before he left for his trip. He asked me to forgive him and wait for him."

"Are you?"

"Momma, as much as I want to believe him, I can't because the trust isn't there anymore and I am afraid he will not change. I love him but I am also scared."

"Torre, living in your own house and scared of your husband is not love. Bible shares in 1 John 4:18, "There is no fear in love but perfect love casts out fear. For fear has to do with punishment and whoever fears has not been perfected in love."

"I know momma but I thought my prayers could change him."

"Who told you that? If prayer could change people, there would be no evil in the world. Girl, God is the only one who can give us the strength and mind to change but it is of our own doing that we do."

"I see that now."

"Better late than never but just know that I am here for you."

"Thanks momma. I love you."

"I love you too baby girl."

We both stand and hug.

"I'm going to get ready for my doctor's appointment. You want to come with me?"

"Of course."

"Good afternoon, I have an appointment with Dr. Meade."

"Your name?"

"Torre Thornton."

"Ok Mrs. Thornton. I need your insurance card and driver's license."

I hand her the requested information and she hands me a packet of information to fill out.

"Once you're done filling those out, bring them back to me while I get your insurance approved."

I finish the paperwork and give it back to the lady. Mom and I sit to chat until they call my name.

After being weighed, peeing in a cup and answering an abundance of questions, I finally change into a gown and wait for the doctor.

== Knock on the door ==

"Hello, my name is Dr. Meade."

"Hi, I'm Torre and this is my mom Katie."

"It is so nice to meet the both of you. Now, what brings you in today?"

"Well, I found out I was pregnant a few weeks ago. It was confirmed while I was in the hospital after a car accident."

"Is that what happened to your wrist?"

"Yes ma'am."

"Do you know the date of your last cycle?"

"I'm not sure because they've never been regular."

"Have you had any prenatal care?"

"No ma'am."

"I will get an ultrasound to make sure the baby is growing and healthy but first, I'm going to lay you back and examine your cervix. It'll be a little pressure but it will give me an estimate of how far along you are."

After a few grunts, Dr. Meade stands up. "Judging by the size of your cervix, you're about 14 to 15 weeks. Let's listen to the heartbeat."

She lifts the gown and rubs this wand type thing over my belly. It takes a minute but the sound of the heartbeat fills the room.

"Oh my God."

I look over at momma and she's crying.

"You can sit up. Everything seems to be fine. You will need to get some bloodwork done, on your way out and I will send prescriptions for prenatal vitamins to your pharmacy but first, I'll have the nurse show you to the ultrasound lab."

"Torre, my name is Tanner and I'll be performing your ultrasound today. Have you ever had an ultrasound?"

"No."

"It will not take long. I'll have you lay back and raise your shirt." He says turning off the light. "Now, I'm going to apply some warm jelly to your stomach then I'll use this wand to see inside. If I am able to tell the sex, would you like to know?"

"Yes."

He begins and after a few minutes, I turn to see the baby on the screen. "This is your baby's heartbeat, it is a strong one, which is very good. I will do a few measurements and then I'll print a few pictures for you." Tanner says.

He does a few more things before wiping the jelly from my stomach. He grabs my hand and helps me up before turning on the light.

He hands me the envelope. I open it.

"It's a girl!" I say to momma.

"Today is September 26, so it puts you right at 15 weeks and this little lady will make her debut around March 17th."

"Oh my God!" I cry. "We're having a little girl."

Daphne

I got a call from Torre saying she's coming to church this morning. It's been a little over a month since Joseph left and even longer since she's been here.

The door opens and I think it's Torre but it turns out to be Carmen.

"Hey, I wasn't expecting you." I say getting up to give her a hug.

"I know but there's something I need to talk to you about."

"Okay."

Before she can say anything, Torre walks in through the back door, I move to hug her.

"Hey! Welcome back, I am so happy to see you."

"Hey girl, how have you been?" She asks.

"Busy but I'm managing."

"I'm sorry to have left everything on you. It was just hard being here after--"

"You don't have to explain. I'm just happy you're here now. Torre this is Carmen. Carmen this is Torre, our First Lady."

"It's nice to meet you." Torre says.

"I know who you are." Carmen says causing me to look at her.

"You do? Are you a member here?"

"No, I used to be married to Joe. I am surprised he never mentioned me."

"Wow, really? When?"

"We divorced a year before you all met."

"How do you know when we met?" Torre asks.

"He told me."

"So you two are still in touch?"

"Yeah, we remained friends even though we made horrible spouses." She laughs but Torre doesn't. "Anyway, I'll get out of the way. Dee, call me later."

"Wait, I thought there was something you wanted to talk about."

"It can wait." She leaves without another word. I turn back to Torre, a little shocked by Carmen's actions.

"Did you know Joe was married before?" She asks me.

"I had no idea."

"How do you know her?"

"I met her at a bar, a few weeks back. I only found out she was married to Joe when she came to see him in the hospital. Is it going to be an issue with us seeing each other?"

"Not at all but why didn't you say anything?"

"Torre, it wasn't my place."

"You're right and I'm sorry. It's just weird he would never mention her, especially if they are friends like she said."

"That's Joe for you but are you sure it isn't going to be a problem?"

"I'm sure. If you're happy, so am I. Are you happy Dee?"

"Yes, I am."

She rubs my face. "Aw, look at you blushing."

I swat her hand away. "I am not. Enough about me, how is your wrist?"

"All good. I just have to wear this wrap for two weeks."

"That's great. Are you staying for service?"

"Yes and speaking of service, how has everything been?"

"Great actually. The speakers Joe lined up have been great and the deacons and trustees have been getting along."

"That's a first." She says laughing.

"I know and God, I pray it stays that way."

"Me too. Is there anything you need me to do while I'm here today?"

"There are some things on your desk that need your attention. With November being two weeks away, the women's committee needs your decision on the nursing home to adopt for Thanksgiving and the community service for December. I sent you an email with all the choices that have been decided on. Once you make your selection, we can get them finalized."

"Thanks Dee."

"Oh, your IPad is in your drawer and Sis. Fisher is hoping you'll let them throw you a baby shower."

"How'd—" She looks at me then laughs.

"I'm sorry Torre but I have her picture on my desk." I say showing her the framed ultrasound. "I can't help it. You know I cannot wait to spoil her, she's my only niece."

She walks over and hugs me.

"I'll let you off the hook this time, only because she is so precious."

"So that's a yes on the shower?"

"Yes."

When she walks to her office, I sit down at my desk before the double doors are pushed open.

What in the Sam hell?"

"I need to speak to Joe."

"Girl, you know he isn't here."

"I know but you can get in touch with him."

"Ana–whatever–your name is, he is on sabbatical which means he is not to be bothered. What do you need?"

"I need the father of my baby to be here when I have this baby."

"And when is that?"

"In two to three weeks."

"Well baby, I can't help you with that."

"What do you mean? You need to call him and call him now! I am not about to have this baby without him. I need pampers, a crib, bottles; hell everything."

I reach into my desk and pull out an envelope, counting out $500 before getting up from my chair.

"Look heifer, you are working on the last nerve I got. Here is five hundred dollars to get whatever you need for that baby. I suggest you make it last until Joe returns because I don't have anything else to give. Now, get your little scrawny ass out of here."

I turn to see Torre standing there.

She shakes her head before closing her office door.

Joseph

Sounds of moans.

"Suck harder. Yea, like that."

She gags before looking up at me and smiling. Another young girl walks from the bathroom and pushes her out the way.

I lay back on the couch as they take turns pleasing me.

"Yes, please daddy." I saw pumping into her mouth.

"Like this?" She asks.

"Yea, spit on it."

"Good girl." The other girl moves up and places a nipple into my mouth.

My phone vibrates.

I push her away. "I need y'all to be quiet."

Pressing answer on the phone. "What's up Dee?"

"Did I wake you? I keep forgetting about the time difference over there."

"No, it's cool, what's wrong?"

"What are you going to do about your baby's mother?"

"Who, Torre?"

"No Negro, Anastasia. She showed up at the church, this morning. I gave her five hundred dollars but I know she'll be back."

"Did you help her find an apartment?"

"Yes."

"Then don't give her nothing else."

"Are you sure because I don't need her causing a scene."

I don't say anything as I watch the two girls please each other.

"Joe, are you there. Hello."

"Shit!" I say when one of them squirts, sending her juices flying across the room.

"Are you okay?"

One of the girls laugh.

"Oh my God." Dee says whispering. "You lying--"

I release the call, throwing the phone into the floor. The girls crawl over to me.

"You okay sir? You aren't hard anymore." She says kissing on my penis.

"Just leave."

"I can try something else."

"No, just get out. Both of you."

I get up from the bed and make sure the door is locked. I close my robe and walk over to the window.

"Damn Dee ruins everything."

My phone vibrates again. I go over and pick it up to see a text from Dee.

DEE: I hope your penis falls off.

ME: Just keep your mouth closed.

DEE: Maybe you should keep your legs closed. BITCH!

Torre

An hour later, I am standing outside the doors preparing to walk into the sanctuary. I am a nervous wreck and my stomach is in knots.

"You alright?" Daphne ask. "You don't have to do this."

"Yea, I'm fine and I need to be here. This is my church too."

She grabs my hand and smile.

The doors open and we walk in. The praise team is up singing, "Your winning season" by Jekalyn Carr. I walk to my usual seat, on the stage but I continue to stand as I join in with worship. I have to believe this is, in fact, my winning season.

When the song is over, Associate Minister Wallace gets up, acknowledging my presence. I stand to wave as the church begins to applaud.

Before I can stop myself, I am walking to the podium.

"Good morning Assembly of God. How are you this morning? God, it feels good to be home."

I pause as the congregation claps so I wait for them to quiet down.

"Please take your seats. I didn't plan on speaking this morning but God has everything ordered." I pause when I feel myself getting emotional. "Listen, I will not stand here and lie like the past months have been good, they haven't. Neither will I act like pastor and I are perfect, we aren't. All I know is, God is good and His mercy endures forever and when His word says, weeping may endure for a night but joy comes in the morning; I surely believe Him. Church, I've had my share of weeping yet here I stand."

"Glory," someone shouts.

"Testify!" Someone else says.

"There were days *and* nights I didn't think I would make it through because the enemy wouldn't leave my home but I'm here. Thank God I am here."

Tears begin to stream down my face. "The person you see today is here only because of God's strength and your prayers. And I believe, with every part of me that He allowed me to go through for somebody else. For somebody who is struggling in their marriage, in their home and even right here in the church. Beloveds, love does not hurt. I don't care who your spouse is, what their job entails or the power they think they have; love does not hurt."

Daphne hands me a handkerchief.

"As women, we have to be strong enough to realize our worth even if it means stepping out of our comfort zone. Please hear me, my husband isn't a bad man but even he has demons that have to be dealt with. Nevertheless, as a body of believers, we have to stop covering up other's fault and pacifying things for an image. There are too many people, right here in the church, who deal with abuse every day. There are people, even in this church, who have their own demons but are afraid to admit it because of the position they hold. Not anymore. Today, men and women, it ends. The silent suffering, the abuse, the lies and the secrets; they end because God is not pleased with us."

I take a breath.

"Assembly of God, I am ashamed of the way I have allowed things to be as your first lady. With you all looking up to me, I have a responsibility to be a role model for those of you who believe in me. I ask one thing of you, don't follow Lady Torre but will you follow the God in me. See, Lady Torre makes mistakes and will sometimes let you down but God never will. Lady Torre may say and do some things unbecoming but God never does and as long as you follow the God in me, you will not be led astray. I love each of you and I pray that you will forgive me for not being here but I'm back where I belong and we will stand in our rightful place, together before God. God bless each of you."

The congregation begins to clap again.

"Now, let's have some church."

Daphne

After service and once everybody is gone, except the cleaning crew, I find myself walking into the sanctuary.

I don't know why but I couldn't bring myself to leave so I sit on a pew, in the middle of the sanctuary with my eyes closed.

"Ms. Daphne, we're done in here. Do you want us to leave the lights on?" Calvin, who is part of the cleaning crew, ask.

"No, you can turn them off. I won't be long."

"Yes ma'am. You have a great day."

"You too."

A few seconds pass before the lights are turned out. It isn't completely dark, because of the sun coming from outside but I don't move.

"I know you're hurt. I know you're torn. I know you are broken but you will win." I sing out loud. "It's my winning season."

"It's my winning season. Everything attached to me wins." I sing. "Everything attached to me has to win." I hit the pew. "Everything has to win. It does."

"Do you believe that?"

I turn to see Torre standing there.

I can't respond.

She sits next to me, placing her hand on my back causing something within me to break and I can no longer control my sobs.

"Dee, it's time for you to be free. You are good at helping everybody else but when will you take the time to help yourself?"

"It's my winning season." I say through the tears hitting the floor.

"You told me that tired people seek rest. Are you not tired? You can't give advice you aren't willing to take."

"It's my winning season." I repeat.

"It can be but you cannot win playing the same game. Get free Dee."

"I don't know how." I scream. "I don't know how."

I get up and walk to the altar where I fall on my knees.

"Oh God, I am sorry. I am so sorry. Please forgive me."

Torre kneels in front of me.

"Let it out Dee."

"OH GOD!" I scream from the depths of my belly. "Please forgive me. I cannot do it on my own anymore. I need you Jesus. Please help me."

I stretch out on the floor sobbing as if a death had just occurred. In a way, death did show up ... to take the old me. This time though, I don't fight instead I willingly hand her over.

I feel Torre's hands rubbing across my back as she begins singing softly, "it's her winning season. It's her winning season. Everything attached to her wins."

Then she prays.

"God, here I am as your servant, humbly asking you to incline your ear to your daughter. God, she is seeking you asking for your forgiveness, grant it. She is seeking you, God, needing your grace because it's only by your grace she can be healed. I know because God, I've been where she is and it doesn't feel good, free her. I've been in the darkness of the pit and know how lonely it can be, comfort her. I've been in the valley and know how rough the nights can be, rock her. Loose now God; the shackles, the burdens, the secrets, the guilt and the anger.

Restore what the locusts have eaten. Return to her your favor. Destroy what circumstances have chained her too. Free now God because she is hungry for you, craving for you to dwell within her. Do it God like only you can. Amen."

I don't know how long I stay in the prostrate position on the altar. All I know is, when I finally open my eyes Torre is still there. And when I get up, she pulls me into her arms with no words to be spoken.

I let out a breath because it feels like a lifetime of weights have been removed from me.

"Thank you," was the only words I could get out.

"No thanks needed. You've always been there for me, it is my turn to be there for you."

4 months later

Joseph

I walk through the airport to baggage claim. I still have a slight limp, from the accident but it is much better. Dee is the only person who knows I'm flying in today and I want to keep it this way.

Anastasia had the baby some months ago and she has been calling, sending texts messages and emails nonstop. To make matters worse, Carmen has been calling too. I had to eventually get a new phone that only Dee and Torre knows of.

I grab my bags and walk over to the Enterprise Rental desk to pick up the truck I'd reserved. My truck was totaled from the accident and although the insurance company has paid the claim, I haven't had time to replace it.

I pull up in my driveway, getting out to punch the code into the garage, since I didn't have an opener. Once I park, I grab my bags before making my way inside, letting the garage back down.

Walking in, I turn off the alarm and turn on a few lights. The staleness of the air lets me know, nobody has been here since I left. I cannot lie, I was praying Torre would be waiting although I knew she wouldn't be.

I've only talked to her a few times since I've been gone and I didn't want to force her to talk to me but I was still holding out hope.

I turn the alarm back on, grab my bags and head down to the bedroom. I undress and shower before putting on some pajama bottoms and sliding under the covers.

The next afternoon, I make the twenty-five minute drive to the apartment complex where Anastasia lives. I park and take the key, Dee left for me and let myself in.

"Joe!" She exclaims running up to me. "When did you get home?"

I have to pry her hands from my neck. "Yesterday."

"Yesterday? And you're just now coming here."

"Tasia, please don't start."

"Fine, you're here now. Come and meet your son."

She grabs my hand pulling me into the bedroom.

"Damn, slow down." I say snatching my hand from her and rubbing my knee.

"My bad baby, I forget about your leg."

She picks him up, handing him to me. "Look at him Joe. He looks just like you."

"What's his name?"

"What do you mean? His name is Joseph Levi Thornton, Jr. Well, I couldn't officially name him a junior because you weren't here to sign the birth certificate but we can always change it later."

"Why would you name him that?"

"He's your son. Your *only* son."

"We don't know that." I say looking at her.

"Joe, please don't come in here acting brand new. We both know you're the only man I've been with. Why are you acting like this?" She asks raising her voice causing the baby to stir.

"Whatever, I don't want to argue with you."

"Fine." She says taking the baby from me.

I walk back up to the living room, looking around the apartment.

"It looks like Dee made sure you have everything you need. The apartment looks nice."

"She wasn't the only one." She hollers from the back.

"What do you mean?"

"Your wife has been helping me too."

I sit on the couch and when I look up, I see her standing there bare ass naked.

"What are you doing?"

"Showing my man how much I missed him."

"Go and put some clothes on."

"But I missed you." She says walking towards me, kneeling. "You've been gone for over four months Joe, I know you missed me, us."

I cannot lie, my penis is throbbing in my pants but I push her away and get up. "No, I am not about to have sex with you. The last thing we need is you getting pregnant again."

"I'm on birth control."

"Yea, you said that last time."

She sighs. "Look Joe, I only want sex, no strings."

"I'm sorry, I cannot help you with that because we both know there are strings when it comes to you."

"What is that supposed to mean?"

"Nothing, I need to get out of here."

"Where are you going? What about your son?"

"I will have my attorney contact you about a paternity test. If he is my son, I will have a visitation schedule set up as well as a monthly allowance to take care of him."

"That's it? What about me?"

"What about you?"

"You said we would be together."

"Look, I said a lot of things I didn't mean and I'm sorry but I cannot be with you. I have too much to lose."

"You weren't caring about that when you were taking my virginity or getting me pregnant."

"You're right and that was a mistake on my part but I will not continue to apologize for it. Like I said, if he is my son I will take care of him but I don't have to be with you to do it. I'm sorry."

"You sure are."

I don't respond as I walk towards the door.

"You're going to regret this!" She screams.

I drive around for a few hours. I stop by the church but I don't go in. I think about going to Dee's house but change my mind.

After driving for a couple more hours, I find myself sitting outside of Ms. Banks' house.

I finally get out of the car and ring the doorbell.

Torre opens it and my eyes instantly go to her stomach area.

"Joe?"

Torre

"Hey, I'm sorry to just show up like this but I wanted to see you and make sure you were okay." Joe says.

"Come in." I step back to let him in. He stops when he sees mom standing there.

"Hey mom, how are you?"

"I am good Joe, how have you been?"

He hesitates but she walks over and gives him a hug.

"I am good."

"Have you been taking care of yourself?" She asks him.

"Yes ma'am, I'm trying."

"That's good. I'll let you and Torre talk. It was good seeing you." She says before walking off.

"Can I get you something to drink?"

"Some water would be good."

He follows me into the kitchen and I motion for him to sit at the table.

"When did you get back? I thought you weren't scheduled to come home until next month."

"I was but I got in yesterday. I realized I needed to be here, with my family."

"Oh." I say handing him a bottle of water.

"Torre, I know I should have called but I was afraid you wouldn't want to see me."

"Why would you think that?"

"Because of everything that has happened."

"Joe, I am not the same woman you left."

"I know and that's why I wanted to talk to you."

"Okay." I sit at the table with him.

"The time away really allowed me to think about a lot of things. First, how are you and the baby?"

"We're good. She's active and healthy."

He smiles. "She?"

"Yes, it's a girl."

"That's great Torre."

"So what do you need to talk about?"

He pauses. "Will you ever forgive me?"

"Joe, I have to forgive you. For my sake and for the baby's."

"I know God says you have to forgive me but what if you didn't. Would you still give me forgiveness for everything I put you through?"

"I would because Joe, in all honesty, you are not a bad person. You simply got comfortable with the conditions you created."

"Do you think you'll ever come back to me?"

"If you'd asked me that a few months back, I wouldn't have been sure but a lot has happened since you've been away."

"You met someone?"

"Actually yes, I met God again."

"Torre, I am being serious right now."

"So am I. While you were gone finding yourself, I spent the same time finding me. See, I had not realized how much of me I'd lost while trying to be everything for you. The sad reality, I didn't even recognize the person I'd become but

I'm different now. I rededicated myself back to God, became more active in the church and I'm stronger Joe."

"Isn't that an even better reason to give us another chance?"

"No, it's a bigger reason of why we shouldn't. I am not the same Torre you left a few months ago."

"Can we at least try?"

"How about we try to get to know each other again in order to be great parents for our daughter?"

"I've known you for the last ten years."

"You knew the old me. The new Torre, you've never met."

"I need you. I need my wife."

"You need the thought of me." I tell him.

He sighs. "Why are you making this so difficult? Can't we just go to counseling or something and start over. I am different now too."

"Yes but the actions of old Joe created a baby with a girl who is barely old enough to drink. So, although you have changed, there are a lot of things you still have to deal with."

"And I will but that doesn't mean we have to give up on our marriage."

"Why didn't you tell me you were married before?"

"What does that have to do with us?"

"Everything! It's another secret you'd been keeping. How do I know there aren't more?"

"It wasn't a secret, it was just something I never discussed."

"Do you know she and Daphne are dating?"

"Yea, I found out before I left."

"And you didn't think to tell me?"

"I'm sorry but that was the furthest thing from my mind. Why are you asking about Carmen? She's a part of my past."

"Not according to the way she reacted when Dee introduced us. Imagine my surprise to be blindsided by the fact my husband was married before and he'd been pillow talking, about me, to her."

"That was the past. Can we leave it there? Daphne doesn't have an issue with it."

"I'm not Daphne, I'm your wife and your nonchalant attitude right now is the very reason we cannot be together."

"Torre, I've apologized for everything already, what more do you want? Yes, Carmen and I were still in contact but it is not how you think."

"Oh enlighten me."

"After we divorced, she started dating women and occasionally, we'd hook up when she needed some male attention. I hadn't seen Carmen in over a year before she called, a few months back."

"So, it didn't matter that you had a wife at home, you were her on-the-go penis to be used whenever she deemed it necessary?"

"No, well yes but baby that's in the past."

"Did you sleep with her the last time she called?"

He hangs his head. "Torre, I am not that person anymore."

"You may not be but you're also not my problem either."

I get up and walk over to the refrigerator, turning back to hand Joe the recent sonogram of our baby.

"She is my biggest priority right now. She's due March 17th and I hope you will be there."

"Two days before my birthday."

"Look Joe, if you don't get yourself together for anyone else, at least do it for the children you've fathered."

Joseph

I stare at the picture for a few minutes and the tears begin to fall from my eyes.

"I really missed things up, didn't I?"

"Yea but now you have a chance to make things right. Although we won't be together as husband and wife, can't we at least be great co-parents?"

I nod my head.

"Have you seen your son?"

"I stopped by there before coming here. She told me you have been sending her money to make sure they are okay. Why would you do that?"

"Joe that little boy is your son and he doesn't deserve to suffer in the midst of this."

"We don't even know if he is."

"That girl is young, naïve and she loves your dirty draws. She told Dee all about her plans for the future and they include you. She isn't dating anybody else because you were the one who took her virginity and sold her the dreams dancing in her head. All you have to do is check her social media page. Joe, he's your son."

I lower my head into my hands. She walks over to me, allowing me to wrap my hands around her stomach.

"I am so sorry Torre and I know I don't deserve you but I do love you. I pray God will send you somebody who will love you better than I could. You are a wonderful woman and will make an even greater mother. I just wish I had the time to make it right for my son and my daughter."

She raises my head.

"Why is this sounding like a goodbye Joe? Is everything okay?"

"I just wanted you to know."

"Joe, what's going on?"

"I need you to do something for me."

"Okay."

"If something happens to me, will you continue to make sure my son is okay? I know it's a lot to ask."

"Nothing is going to happen to you."

"I know but I've made a lot of mistakes and it is only a matter of time before they come back to bite me. I just feel like death is looming near."

"Don't talk like that. God has given you the ability to handle a lot of storms, this will be no different. All you have to do is be willing to change and open to getting the help you need."

"I love you Torre."

"I love you too and we will get through this."

I stand up and she hugs me. When I pull back, she allows me to kiss her. For the first time in a long time, I kiss her before pulling her back into a hug. I linger there and she doesn't rush me to let her go and I don't because this time, it feels different.

It feels like goodbye.

"Will you stay and have dinner with us? Momma fixed greens and fried chicken."

"You sure? I don't want to intrude."

"Nonsense, you won't be intruding." Her mom says walking into the kitchen. "Besides, looking at you, you could use a good home cooked meal."

Looking down at myself, I realize how right she was.

"Then, I'd love too."

After dinner, I sit around and talk with Torre and her mom for hours. Before we realize it, it's after eleven.

Torre's mom offer to let me sleep in the guest room but I decide to go home. I give each of them a hug and I kiss Torre goodbye, promising to go to her doctor's appointment in a few days.

I make it to the car, sitting there a few minutes watching Torre at the door before pulling off. Stopping at a light, I reach into my pocket and turn my phone back on.

As soon as it powered up, it rings with a call from Carmen.

"Carmen?"

"Joe, why haven't you been answering my calls?"

"You knew I was in India. I just got back."

"And? I bet you answered everybody else who called you."

"Look, what's up? I am tired and not in the mood."

"I need to talk to you."

"Whatever it is will have to wait until tomorrow. I'm going home."

"Can I come there?"

"NO! Did you not just hear me say I am tired? I will call you tomorrow."

Daphne

I've been sitting in front of my computer for the last hour, trying to type a resignation letter. Valentine's Day is tomorrow and the church is having a couple's ball so I figured, I'd make it my last event as Pastor Joe Thornton's admin.

He has been back from India for a few days now but I haven't answered any of his calls. Now, as I sit here to type this letter, I cannot find the words.

I get up and begin walking in circles, praying out loud.

"Dear God, whose name is holy and sweet. Thank you for daily bread, for grace and for mercy. God, I thank you for the assignment you've allowed me to serve in but if it is time for me to move, please show me. I am tired, oh God, and my spirit is in turmoil that only you can heal. Show me what you will have me to do because I cannot do it on my own. If it is time to end this covenant relationship and if my work here is done, sever it because I don't have the strength to do it. I know you can God. Amen."

After a few minutes, I sit down and begin to type.

"Joe,

This is my letter of resignation, to you. I have an official letter to be submitted to the deacon board but there are some things I need to personally tell you. Man, you are a piece of work. You don't care about anyone or anything unless it's for your satisfaction. Over the years, I've seen you destroy the lives of young girls you had no business being with and I pray you don't ever get back half the shit you deserve. Yes, I had a hand in it by covering up your misdeeds and for that only God can forgive me.

This is why, after ten years, it is time for me to remove myself from this derailing train. I know you are not entirely to blame because I could have left at any time but I will not dwell on the past. I have to do what is best for me and that is to disconnect myself from you.

As for you, I hope and pray the time you spent in India gave you the peace you need to finally get help. For your sake as well as for Torre and your children. She is a great woman and she doesn't deserve the hell you've put her through and I pray she finds somebody else who loves her like you couldn't. I pray you will find someone else, preferably a man, who can fill the shoes I am leaving behind because we all know you don't need a woman. Anyway, thank you for the years but this time I am choosing my sanity over your secrets.

– Dee.

The sound of the doorbell stops me. I save what I have so far and close the laptop.

"Who is it?"

"It's Carmen."

I turn off the alarm and open the door.

"Hey, I come bearing gifts." She says holding up a bottle of wine.

I step back to let her in.

"I am surprised to see you since I haven't laid eyes on or talked to you since that Sunday at the church."

"I know and I'm sorry. There were some things I had to deal with on my own."

"That's understandable but not even a text or return phone call? I know we weren't in a relationship or anything but for you to just up and fall off the grid was crazy."

"I know but I am here now, hoping to make it up to you."

"How?"

She walks up to me.

"Wait, as much as I want to have sex with you, it will not make everything better."

She steps back. "You're right. It was inconsiderate of me to ignore your calls and text but I was beginning to catch feelings for you and I didn't know how you'd react knowing you're so close to Joe and his wife."

"Then you should have talked to me because then you'd know everything is different."

"Different?"

"I'm resigning."

"Resigning? Why?"

"It's long overdue. I love Joe but it's time I move on." I say getting emotional.

"If you are getting emotional talking about it, I highly doubt you'll be able to go through with it."

"Oh, I am because if I don't, things will probably end with one of us having an early death and the other being in prison."

"Have you talked to Joe? Does he know?"

"Not yet. I plan on telling him tomorrow at the Valentine's gala."

"So you still have your keys?"

"My keys? What does that have to do with anything?"

"Uh, I was asking in case you need some help cleaning out your office."

"I'm not leaving the church, I'm just stepping down as his admin. Anyway, is this what you came here to talk about?"

"No, I came to apologize. I'm sorry." She says kissing me.

"Hmm, how sorry are you?"

"Let me show you."

"No, stop, I can't." I say pushing her away.

"Please Daphne. Just one more time and then we never have to see each other again, if you don't want too."

I hesitate for a minute. "Fine but this is the last time, I'll meet you in the bedroom. It's down the hall on the right."

I make sure the door is locked before I walk back to the bedroom. She walks in front of me and has already removed her clothes. I quickly remove my shirt, turning around for her to undo my bra.

Sliding out of my leggings, I push them off with my feet.

I walk over to pull the comforter and sheet all the way down to the end of the bed.

"Lay down." I order.

"Oh, you're in charge now?"

"Yep. My house, my rules."

She sits on the bed.

"Do you trust me Carmen?"

"Yes."

"Good, lay back."

I walk over to the bottom drawer on the dresser and pull out some scarves. I move around, tying her to the bed posts before going into the kitchen to get some ice.

"What are you doing?" She asks when I walk into the bedroom.

"You'll will see." I say sitting the cup on the nightstand.

I straddle her and place the last scarf over her eyes before tracing her lips with my tongue.

She moans.

I kiss her neck before moving down to her chest where I spend ample time getting to know each one of her breast.

She moans louder.

I move down to her stomach, stopping at her belly button.

She moans even louder.

When I reach the top of her vagina, I pause, running my hand over the clean shaven area.

Blowing on her, she bucks. I look at her to see that she's biting her lip.

I lean over, on the nightstand, and take a cube of ice into my mouth, allowing the water to drop on her.

"Oh," she coos.

Rubbing the ice over my lips, I kiss her on her lips; the ones below.

"Shiiittt!"

I take another ice cube into my mouth before spreading her lips and allowing the cool water to cover her. Using my thumb, I massage her clit, sliding it in between her lips as she moans my name. When the ice melts, I suck her clit into my mouth, slowly allowing my tongue to explore every part of her.

"God, your tongue feels good. Let me taste you. Please."

I smile before turning to where we are now in a 69 position.

"Untie my hands." She begs.

"You don't need your hands, just your tongue. Ahh yeah, just like that."

I resume my tasting of her as she cries out from the orgasm.

I don't give her time to recover as I remove the scarf from her left leg, maneuvering her into a position so our vaginas meet.

As I begin to ride her, I bend her leg, taking her toes into my mouth.

Her cries get louder as we climax together before I collapse on the bed beside her.

"Remove these." She says breathing hard.

I lay back on the bed with my eyes closed until I feel her getting up.

"You leaving?" I ask her.

"No, I'm going to get the bottle of wine because we're in for a long night."

Joseph

"Amen."

I get up off my knees after finishing my prayers. I take a shower and put on a pair of pajamas pants before going into the kitchen to make a drink.

After grabbing my IPad and cell phone, I walk back into the bedroom to finish the sermon I've been working on in preparation for my first Sunday back, in a few weeks.

I open the bible app to 1st Peter 4:12–14 and begin reading out loud.

"Dear friends, don't be surprised at the fiery trials you are going through, as if something strange were happening to you. Instead, be very glad--for these trials make you partners with Christ in his suffering, so that you will have the wonderful joy of seeing his glory when it is revealed to all the world. So be happy when you

are insulted for being a Christian, for then the glorious Spirit of God rests upon you."

I hit record on my voice notes.

"Sermon prep. 1st Peter, chapter four, verses twelve through fourteen. Sermon is going to be titled, the cost of the oil."

After working for another few hours, I yawn, realizing how tired I am. I plug my phone into the charger and place it on the night stand. Closing out the apps I'd been using on my IPad, I open Safari.

In the search bar, I type in Porn Hub and press go. When the page loads, I search my favorite category of videos to find the one I'm looking for. Pressing play, I get comfortable in the bed before I slide my hand into my pajama pants to massage myself.

A few hours later, I jolt from my sleep when I feel somebody touching me.

"What are you doing here?"

"You know I could have helped you with this." She says rubbing my penis that is still hanging out of my pants.

I cover myself and she takes the IPad that had fallen beside me.

"It figures you'd be watching porn. I guess the saying is true, you can't teach an old dog new tricks."

"How did you get in my house?"

"These," she says dangling keys. "And you forgot to turn on your alarm. Very stupid mistake."

"Where did you get those?"

"That doesn't matter. Now get up."

"I'm not doing shit. Get out of my house."

"No can do because tonight I'm in charge boo." She says pulling out a gun. "Now, get the fuck up!"

"Fine!" I say throwing the comforter back but not getting up.

"Do you think you can just continue to lie and manipulate people?"

I laugh. "Oh, I guess you think you're a victim?"

"I am. I'm a victim of Pastor Joseph Levi Thornton, Sr."

"Baby, you cannot be mad at me for catching feelings when you knew who I was and what you were getting."

"Do you think this is a joke?"

I stand up to put my penis back in my pants. When I look up, she's staring at my crotch so I drop my pants and rub him. "If he's what you want, all you have to do is ask. You know he still gets hard for you. Why don't you put the gun down and come show daddy some love."

She moves closer to me.

"Why couldn't you love me Joe?"

I extend my hand to her. "Just give me the gun and we can talk about it."

"You promise?" She asks walking closer.

"Yes baby, I promise."

When I reach for the gun, she swings, clipping my chin.

"Did you actually think I'd fall for that?"

"You used too." I laugh.

"Not anymore. All these months, I've tried to get your attention. I called, you ignore me. I give the health department your name and you even ignore it. When you do show up, you fuck me like I'm a common whore."

"You are not making sense. Why would you give me my name to the health department?"

"Because I thought you'd come back to me."

"You crazy bitch!"

"You made me crazy. You didn't want my baby but you turn around and get that whore pregnant."

"Baby?"

"It should have been me!" She screams. "I was supposed to be your wife."

"And standing in my house with a gun is going to solve that for you?"

"Did you know my daddy died Joe?" She asks sounding like a child.

"Your daddy--how would I know that?"

"You remember that day I called you and you didn't come? He died that day. Why didn't you come Joe?" She screams.

"What does your father's death have to do with any of this?"

"He said I messed everything up by letting you go. He said you were the meal ticket we needed. I tried to explain it to him but he wouldn't listen to me."

"Explain what to him?"

"That you reminded me of him."

"Baby you're not making sense. Please put the gun down and let us talk about this."

"I tried to tell him Joe. I wanted him to know the way you smelled, the way you touched me and even the way you used to look at me reminded me of him but he wouldn't listen."

"I don't understand."

"You loved me like my father!"

I look at her with a face full of disgust.

"Don't look at me like that. He was all I ever had."

"Okay but what does this have to do with me, now?"

"You're all I have left. Now that he's gone, I need you."

"I am not your daddy."

"Yes you are." She smiles. "You talk just like him. All you have to do is divorce that bitch and marry me."

"I am not doing that."

"YES.YOU.ARE." She says raising the gun. "My daddy told me, before he died, to get you back and that's what I'm here to do."

I look over at my phone on the nightstand.

"Don't even think about it Joe. This doesn't have to be hard."

"What's your end goal? You cannot possibly think I will marry you just because you say I have too. Look, I am sorry for all the things I've done to you and everybody else but I am not that person anymore. I am trying to do better and right my relationship with God. I can't do that with you."

"Blah, blah. My end goal is to death do us part."

"Think about what you're saying. It's obvious you're having some kind of psychotic break. Why don't you put the gun down so we can talk and get you some help, please?"

"We don't need to talk and I don't need help. All I need you to say is, you will be mine either in life or death."

"I will not agree to that and if I have to die tonight, I'm ready."

She begins to walk in circles. The second her back is to me, I yell out--

"Hey Siri." When I hear the beep. "Call the police."

Siri says, "Calling Dee."

"No!" She screams before rushing to get the phone. I try to push her out the way but it causes us to tussle.

"Aw," I scream when the gun connects to my face. I drop to my knees.

When she sees the blood, she stumbles back and cries, "Oh God." Realizing she's gone too far, she hits me again until I black out.

Daphne

Sound of my phone vibrating

"Ah shit," I say feeling around for my phone, finally touching it on the nightstand.

"Hello." I answer barely opening my eyes.

Nobody says anything.

"Hell-lo!" I say blinking a few times to see the caller id clearer.

"Joe?" I blow into the phone.

Sounds of shuffling.

"Aw," someone says.

What in the entire hell? "Joe?"

"Oh God!" A woman's voice says.

I know this bastard did not call me while having sex. I call his name again. When I hear what sounds like the phone dropping, I sit up in the bed.

"JOE!"

Still nothing so I release the call before dialing his number back.

No answer.

Shaking my head.

I put the phone back on the nightstand before grabbing the cup sitting there and swallowing all the water in it.

I look around the room, thankful to at least be at home because I cannot, for the life of me, remember what in the hell happened. I see scarves laying on the bed and a wine bottle on the floor but wine has never left me feeling like this.

I swing my legs over the edge of the bed and stand up but when my feet touch the floor, I stagger.

I close my eyes and hold my head to stop the swirling. "Oh God."

I barely make it to the toilet, before emptying my stomach contents.

I sit there a minute trying to get myself stable enough to stand up. Finally pulling up to the sink, I turn on the water, hoping the coldness will sober me up.

It doesn't.

I rinse my mouth and look at my reflection trying to remember something, anything about the night.

I sigh.

Walking back to the bedroom, my foot kicks the wine bottle. I bend down to pick it up when my eyes focus in on my purse that's open on the floor.

I sit the bottle on the dresser and reach for my purse only to see keys laying on top of it. I raise them up and realize the second key chain that hold keys for Joe's house, the church and my desk are gone.

I rush over to grab my phone, dialing Joe's number.

"Answer! Come on Joe!"

No answer.

I try again. "Damn it! Come on Joe, answer the freaking phone."

When he still doesn't answer, I send a text.

"Joe, please call me. I think you're in trouble."

I lay the phone down and grab the cup from the nightstand to get more water. After walking out the bathroom, I pick up my phone to see Joe still hasn't responded, so I call him again.

No answer.

"Lord, please let this man be okay."

Carmen

I bend down and grab the phone but the call ended.

"FUCK!" I scream.

I look at the phone and see that it dialed Daphne's number. She calls back so I press decline.

Joe is laying on the floor so I sit against the bed and pull his head into my lap. I caress his face.

"You didn't have to make this hard Joe. All I wanted was you. I needed you to take care of me like daddy did."

I close my eyes and when I open them again, I see daddy's face instead of Joe's.

"What have you done?"

"I tried to get him daddy because I need him to make me feel like you used too but he wouldn't listen."

"What are you going to do now? He will never love you like I did, not after this."

"Then I'll kill him."

I close my eyes again and this time when I open them, he's gone. I look down at Joe and he begins to moan.

"Carm--"

"Shh." I say rubbing his face.

"I," cough, "need," cough, "help."

"I know."

"Please." He says as his phone rings again.

"Go away Daphne." I say hitting decline. She calls again before sending a text. "Joe, please call me. I think you're in trouble."

"Yes Daphne, he's in trouble but you won't be able to save him this time."

He moans again.

"Hush little baby, don't you cry. Carmen is going to make sure tonight you die."

I push his head away, just enough to press the gun against his temple.

"Forgive him Father for he knows not what he was doing." I laugh before pulling the trigger causing the blood to splatter all over my face and chest.

I drop the gun before rubbing his face and rocking.

The sound of his phone causes me to jump.

"Damn Daphne, do you ever go away?" I scream. "Well since you can't seem to leave us the fuck alone, why don't you join us?"

I send her a text from Joe's phone.

ME: Dee, I need your help.

DEE: Haven't you seen my calls? Why won't you answer the phone?

ME: I cannot talk. I need you to come.

DEE: Come where?

ME: My house.

DEE: Is it Torre?

"FUCK NO!" I yell before replying.

ME: No, just come, please!

DEE: I'm on the way but you better not have another woman in that house!

I laugh. "Oh he definitely has another woman in the house."

I slide Joe's body from my lap and get up.

"I guess Ms. Daphne will have to take the fall for your death Joe. It'll be sad because she is a great lay, I mean lady but oh well. The police will find her resignation letter and think all of this became too much for her and she killed you. Yes, that's a great idea Carmen."

I walk up front and turn on the light in the living room because I didn't want her to think something was wrong. Walking back to the bedroom, Joe's phone vibrates with another text from Daphne.

"Joe, something doesn't feel right so I am sending the police."

"NO! NO! NO! NO! Why do you always mess stuff up?" I yell throwing the phone into the wall.

I pace around the room trying to think of a way out. After a few minutes, I kneel down beside Joe and kiss him on the lips before moving down to kiss his penis one last time. "Damn, I'm going to miss the both of you but I guess I'll see you in the afterlife."

I pick up the gun and put it to my head.

Daphne

After going back and forth with text from Joe, I walk over to the dresser and grab some underwear. I stop when it feels like I'll be sick again but closing my eyes and taking a few deep breathes help. When I open them, I see the wine bottle again and it hits me, this bitch drugged me.

I quickly slip on some panties and a bra before putting on a pair of pajama pants, a sweatshirt and UGG Boots.

Grabbing my purse, I get to the car and push the start button. My hand grabs the gear shift to put it in reverse but I stop because something doesn't feel right. I try to call Joe again but he doesn't answer so I make another call.

"911, what's your emergency?"

"Uh, yes I think my boss is in trouble."

"In trouble how ma'am?" The dispatcher asks.

"I don't know but can you please send somebody just to check?"

"I can but it'll be a minute before I can get a car there unless there is something else going on?"

"I can't explain it ma'am but he sent a text asking me to come to his house but now he won't answer my calls. I really believe he is in danger."

"What's the address ma'am?"

"1001 Fen Bark Hollow in Cordova."

"The name of the person you believe to be in trouble?"

"Joseph Thornton."

"And your name?"

"Daphne Gary."

"We will have a car sent."

"Please hurry."

I hang up and send a text.

"Joe, something doesn't feel right so I am sending the police."

Twenty minutes later, I hurriedly pull in front of Joe's house and get out. There is a police car in the driveway so I rush to the door. When I get there, the door is pushed opened and I see an officer standing inside.

"What's going on?"

"Ma'am, you can't go any further." He says stopping me in the living room.

I look around but I don't see Joe and the only other light on is in the master bedroom.

"This is my boss' house. I am the one who called for the welfare check so can you please tell me what's going on?"

"Ma'am, you will need to wait outside."

"Joe!" I scream. "Joe! Please just tell me what is happening."

"I cannot give you any information. If you wait outside, a detective will be here to speak to you."

I turn, acting like I'm headed outside but instead I push pass him running towards the master bedroom. Getting to the door, my heart drops into my stomach at the scene.

"Oh my God, no!" I cry as the officer pulls me out the room and into the living room.

"You will need to stay here." He says as the sounds of sirens fill the streets.

"Are they – are they dead?" I ask through tears as EMTs run in.

"Ma'am, please just stay here."

A few minutes later, they walk out shaking their head at the officer who gets on his radio. "Dispatch, we have a 10–70 at my location. Roll a homicide detective and crime scene."

"NOO!" I scream. "This cannot be happening." "Oh God, Joe!"

- - - - -

I open my eyes to a gentleman next to me, I jump up.

"Whoa, ma'am, calm down."

"What happened?"

"You passed out."

I look around and realize it wasn't a nightmare and I begin to cry.

"Ma'am, my name is Detective Alton Jeffrey. What is your name?"

"Daphne Gary."

"Are you the one who called 911?"

"Yes."

"Why did you suspect something was wrong here tonight?"

"I don't know, a gut feeling I had."

"A feeling?"

"Sir, I cannot explain it but can you just tell me what happened?"

"We are still investigating." He says. "When you called 911, you said the owner of this house is--"

"Joseph Thornton." I answer.

"Does he live alone?"

"Yes, his wife moved out a few months ago."

"And how did he contact you tonight?"

"Text."

"How long ago?"

"I don't know, my phone is in my car but I guess about an hour ago."

He looks at his watch.

"Oh God, Torre." I cry.

"Who is Torre?"

"His wife."

"The other victim is --"

"That's not his wife." I respond, cutting him off.

"How can you be so sure?"

"The clothes she has on. I know who that is."

"Ms. Gary--"

I hear him talking but his words are not registering because my eyes are watching the coroner and crime scene crew who have just arrived.

"Oh God," I cry. "She's going to be so devastated."

"Ms. Gary, I know this is hard but I need to know how to get in touch with Mrs. Thornton."

"Yes, um, she's staying with her mom in Millington. Her phone number is, 9016547445."

"Thank you. I may have some additional questions so I'm going to have an officer escort you down to homicide."

He motions for an officer to come over.

"Can I get my purse out the car?"

"Yes but I have to ask you not to make any phone calls until we've had ample time to notify the family."

Torre

Walking from the bathroom, I sit on the side of the bed. There is a feeling in the pit of my stomach that I just cannot seem to shake. I've been praying since 2:30 this morning.

I start to get back under the cover when I see the light from my phone, on the nightstand.

"Hello."

"I apologize for calling at this hour however, I am trying to reach Mrs. Torre Thornton?"

"This is Torre."

"Mrs. Thornton, my name is Detective Alton Jeffrey with the Memphis Police Department. Again, I'm sorry to wake you but it is imperative that I speak to you."

"Its fine detective, I was awake. What is this about?"

"Your husband. Is it possible for me to come and speak to you now?"

"My husband? Is he in trouble?"

"Ma'am, I'd much rather discuss this in person. I can either come to you or have a car pick you up and bring you to the station."

"Here is fine. I'm at my mother's house." I say giving him the address.

After releasing the call, I get out of bed to wake mom. I tap on her door.

"Mom?"

"What's wrong? Is it the baby?" She asks sitting up.

"No ma'am, it's Joe."

"Joe? What's wrong with him?"

"I don't know but the police are on the way to speak to me."

An hour later, I am pacing in the living room when the doorbell rings. I rush over to open the door.

"Mrs. Thornton?"

"Yes, please come in."

"I'm Detective Alton Jeffrey and this is my partner Detective Essence Harrison."

I step back to let them in. "This is my mom Katie Banks. Please have a seat. You said this is about Joe, what happened?"

"Ma'am, a Memphis 911 dispatcher received a call a few hours ago requesting a welfare check on your husband because she believed him to be in some kind of trouble."

"What kind of trouble?"

"She didn't know." He says.

"Well, who made the call?"

"A woman by the name of Daphne Gary."

"Okay, that's Joe's Admin. Why would she think he was in trouble?"

"She said it was gut feeling." The other detective answers. "Ma'am, when officers arrived on the scene your husband and a female victim were located in the master bedroom of the home. They were both deceased."

I hear the words but they don't register.

"I apologize, I don't think I heard you correctly. Please repeat what you said. I saw your lips moving but—please say that again."

"I am sorry to have to tell you but your husband was a victim of a crime tonight and he did not survive."

My mother gasps.

"A victim of a crime? Where?"

"At his residence. A preliminary investigation is leaning towards a murder suicide." Detective Jeffrey says."

"This doesn't make sense. Murder-suicide? Who would do this?"

"A car located outside the residence is registered to a Ms. Carmen Thornton. Do you know who she is?"

"His ex-wife but why would Carmen kill Joe?"

"We are still early in the investigation so we cannot answer that. We were hoping you could shed some light on their relationship."

"Detectives, I wish I could but my husband was a liar and deceiver. I only recently found out he had an ex-wife so you will probably find out the reason behind all of this before I can."

"How long were you and Mr. Thornton married?"

"Ten years." I reply wiping the tears sliding down my face.

"And you never knew he had an ex-wife?"

"There are a lot of things I didn't know about my husband. Where is Daphne? She knows him better than anyone."

"Why do you say that?" Detective Harrison asks.

"She was his admin and she kept his secrets. If anybody knows Joe, it's her. Where is she?"

"She is down at the homicide department."

"What happens now detective? Can I see Joe? His body, I mean?"

"Yes, you will receive a call from the medical examiner's office in order to make a positive identification of your husband's body sometime tomorrow. I am sorry for your loss. You and your family has my deepest condolences."

Two Weeks Later

Celebrating the Life and Legacy

Of

Joseph Levi Thornton

March 19, 1979 – February 14, 2018

Assembly of God Christian Center

14785 Assembly Way

Memphis, TN 38111

Dr. Aubrey Wainwright, Officiating

His Life, His Time, His Legacy

"To everything there is a season and a time to every purpose under the Heaven." – Ecclesiastes 3:1

His Life ...

"But even before I was born, God chose me and called me by His marvelous grace. Then it please him." Galatians 1:15

Joseph Levi Thornton was born into this world on March 19, 1979 in Brentwood, TN as the only son to the late George and Thelma Thornton.

He accepted God into his life and became a member of Springhill MB Church in Brentwood until God called him to pastoral leadership. He married his soul mate, Torre, with whom he was expecting his first daughter.

His Time ...

"Whatever you do, work heartily, as for the Lord and not for men." Colossians 3:23

Joseph was a hard worker who dedicated over 15 years to the call of God on his life. He graduated from Carter Seminary with a degree in Biblical Studies and Stroll College with a Certificate of Pastoral Counseling. Joseph has received numerous awards for his tireless work in the community and for serving on the board of Memphis Children's Hospital.

During his tenure as pastor, Joseph had the privilege of pastoring two Memphis churches before becoming the founder of Assembly of God Christian Center in 2013.

Joseph will be remembered for his love of God, his work in the community and his adoration for this church and God's people.

His Legacy ...

"A good man leaves an inheritance to his children's children ...." Proverbs 12:22

Joe leaves to carry his legacy, his wife Torre. A son, Joseph Jr., his unborn daughter and his mother-in-love Katie Banks. As well as his church family, friends and a community of believers. He will also be missed by his Admin whom he affectionately called Dee, Ms. Daphne Gary.

Torre

I take a deep breath when I make it to the podium. I look out over the sanctuary and it is standing room only.

"This is the hardest thing I have ever experienced. I never would have imagined I'd be standing here when just a few days ago, my life was as normal as it could be, unaware the next moment I'd be forced into the shoes of a widow. And man, are they are heavy."

"As much as I want to question God, how can I? How can I be mad at Him for coming back to take who rightfully belongs to Him? How can I be upset at God for repossessing what He owns? The bible says in James 4:14, yet you do know what tomorrow will bring. What is your life? For you are a mist that appears for a little time and then vanishes."

I pause to swallow the emotions that are threatening to spill from the depths of my soul.

"While I am grateful to each of you who showed up this afternoon, sent food, flowers, called and even prayed for our family; I cannot leave here without telling each of you, you don't have time. We make preparations for the future and we make plans for tomorrow but what are we doing with the time we have right now? What are we doing with the minutes we have at this very moment?"

"Believers of God, stop taking life and people for granted. My husband is gone, there is no need to eulogize him but I would not be who God has called me to be if I did not take this moment to possibly save somebody under the sound of my voice."

"Because whether we want to admit it; demons, spiritual battles, mental illness and suicide are all real. Stop suffering in silence. Stop being afraid to ask for help. If you or someone you know is suffering, with whatever it is, seek help. Don't wait until it's too late to deal with the things that torment you because you don't have time. You don't have time to wait because you may not see tomorrow."

"And please, please hear me well. Just because someone looks like they have it all together, they could be a hug away from a mental breakdown. Pay attention to those you love, ask questions and pick up the phone to hear their voice. Don't take a second for granted because life is just a vapor."

"I don't know what tomorrow holds but I will do my best to carry on Joe's legacy, especially the one he had for Assembly of God. Just because he has now taken his rest does not mean we close the doors. If anything, we have to work even harder to make sure no one else suffers because then his death will be in vain."

"Again, I thank each of you and in the minutes, days, weeks and months to come when you've gone back to the normalcy of your life;

whisper our name in prayer because we will definitely need it."

"May the God we serve bless each of you with the abundance of grace you stand in need of."

I turn to Daphne who is standing right beside me. I grab her hand and smile as we walk back to our seats.

After the service, we pile into the limousine heading to the cemetery. I look over at Anastasia who is with us in the family car. I really didn't care about the stares and the whispers, I asked her to ride with us because she has Joe's son and I cannot deny him or her. I reach over to touch her, getting her attention. She smiles at me before looking down to the baby as he sleeps in her lap.

When the car comes to a stop, I put my shades on and take a deep breath as the door opens.

I sit in the chair and watch Joe's casket as Pastor Wainwright speaks. I am lost in my thoughts when Daphne taps my hand, giving me a flower.

We walk up together as the pastor reads, John 14:27-28, "Peace I leave with you, my peace I give you. I do not give to you as the world gives. Do not let your hearts be troubled and do not be afraid. You heard me say, 'I am going away and I am coming back to you.' If you loved me, you would be glad that I am going to the Father, for the Father is greater than I."

"You may now place your flowers on the casket." She says.

I place my flower there but I cannot bring myself to remove my hand. I bend over the casket and allow my tears to cover it as pastor continues.

"Forasmuch as it hath pleased Almighty God of his great mercy to take unto himself the soul of our dear brother, we therefore commit his body to the ground; earth to earth, ashes to ashes, dust to dust; in sure and certain hope of the Resurrection to eternal life, through our Lord Jesus Christ; who shall change our vile body, that it may be like unto his glorious body, according to the mighty working, whereby he is able to subdue all things to himself. Amen."

I turn to face Daphne, who pulls me into a hug.

"We will be alright, won't we?" I ask her.

"We have no choice but to be."

Epilogue

Daphne

Today is the first day I have opened my computer since the night everything happened.

It's been almost three weeks.

When it powers on, the first thing that comes up is my resignation letter. I immediately start to cry before pushing the computer away.

I sometimes find myself looking at the door to Joe's office and wondering if he'd still be alive if he and things were different. I have so many what ifs.

What if I never gave Carmen access to me, what if she wouldn't have been able to get the keys to Joe's house, what if Joe would have been a better person and what if he was faithful instead of a hoe?

I know the 'what ifs' will drive me crazy but that's why I'm in therapy now. She, my therapist, is working to teach me how to forgive myself because at the end of all this, it wasn't my fault.

Besides, what I now know about Carmen, she would have gotten to him anyway, with or without my help. See, during the investigation, the police found a diary Carmen kept and it was mind blowing, chilling and downright horrific. The contents of that diary makes the hair stand up on the back of your neck.

Carmen was certifiable crazy. The padded room, 24 hour guard, medicated with an electronic ankle bracelet kinds of crazy.

We found all of this out with the help of Detective Jeffrey, who was great about keeping us updated on the details of the case. He knew we needed closure and it only came by rationalizing why Carmen did what she did.

Although Joe had his faults, he did not deserve to die in the manner he did. The saddest part of all this, no one saw it coming, not even me.

Anyway, back to Crazy Carmen. As it would turn out, Carmen knew who I was the entire time and our meeting at the bar was not a coincidence. In her diary, she only referred to me as Joe's "Olivia Pope."

I remember her saying it, the day at Joe's house but I laughed it off because it was funny not knowing she really meant it.

Baby, she meant every letter because this chick was obsessed with Joe. No, not the save a few pictures her and there; she was the Lifetime Movie Network kind of obsessed. Her obsession was made worse with her and Joe's sexual relationship.

I know you're asking, why didn't someone notice? But she was good at managing her crazy.

Things only got worse when her daddy, whom she called "Daddy Bear," died about seven months ago.

In her diary, she explained how she became everything her daddy needed, after the passing of her mom, in 2005, from an aneurysm. Understand me ... when I say she became everything, I mean EV–VER–RE–THING!

We still cannot figure out how she was married to Joe and he not see the signs but I guess if you aren't looking for them, you'll miss them. Anyway, she and Joe married in 2003 and divorced in 2006. He then went on to meet and marry Torre in 2007.

Nevertheless, after the death of her Daddy Bear, she needed Joe because he reminded her of him. She had it all planned out and no was an answer she was determined not to accept.

The day she called him over to her house and they had sex in the truck, *yes she wrote about it*, was the day she started planning their new wedding. NO LIE.

The house she stayed in, she had not changed a thing. It was as if her daddy was still there. His clothes were hanging in the closet, his shoes were next to the bed, his glasses on the nightstand, his place was sat at the table and all his favorite foods were in the refrigerator.

The chick had every intention on turning Joe into her Daddy Bear.

A few problems.

Anastasia and the baby.

Torre.

Me.

Oh yes, she accounted for that too. She had written out plans to kill everybody but me. She needed me alive for the design to work but Joe's confession and trip to "find himself" threw a wrench in her plans.

Then he came home early, which further complicated things. So, she had to go to plan B. It almost worked but Joe's phone called me that night and I am glad it did because it saved a lot of lives.

Thank you Jesus!

Needless to say, it has been a rough few weeks but we are on the mend.

As for me, I am leery about meeting anybody. I have even resolved to run background checks on anybody I don't know.

What? You can never be too careful.

Anastasia is doing great. She is now in college and working while raising the baby, who is getting so big.

Torre is adamant about raising him and her daughter together. I commend her for that because I don't know if I could look at the woman my husband had an affair with, almost every day.

But hey, she has a much bigger and forgiving heart than I do.

Before I forget, Mallory Grace Thornton was born on her daddy's birthday, March 19, 2018. She weighed five pounds and three ounces and she is beautiful.

Torre is on the mend, as well, as she has a church to run and a family to raise.

As for the church, we are holding on. Torre, who now holds the governing reigns, recently started the search process for a new pastor.

As for me. Yes, I am still in my position as admin but now I report only to Torre. I am done with being the admin to any other pastor, male or female.

PERIOD!

Chile, his secrets almost cost me my sanity and it is no longer up for sale!

I hope you have enjoyed reading The Pastor's Admin. If you did, please leave a review and recommend it.

As always, when I write, I pray it helps someone. If you are going through, dealing with abuse (of any kind), fighting spiritual demons; please get help. You don't have to suffer in silence because God wants his children to be free and that means free from everything that binds us.

Bible shares in *Galatians 5:1, "For freedom Christ has set us free; stand firm therefore, and do not submit again to a yoke of slavery."*

What's slavery? An excessive dependence on or devotion to something. In other words, making yourself a bondservant to something or somebody who means you no good. Nothing should have a hold on you.

Get free beloved. Make this season your winning season because you deserve to be happy. Find your happiness.

I have a devotional journal titled, HEROINE Addict: Journaling your way to becoming addicted to the heroine you are. This is for women to use as a tool to becoming the she-ro, the noble woman and the HERoine you are. It's not too late and don't allow anyone to convince you that it is.

Again, I thank you for taking the time to read my work! I cannot express what it means to me every time you support me!

For upcoming contests and give-a-ways, I invite you to like my Facebook page, AuthorLakisha, follow my blog authorlakishajohnson.com or join my reading group Twins Write 2.

If this is your first time reading my work, please slide over to Amazon and check out the many other books available:

A Secret Worth Keeping

A Secret Worth Keeping: Deleted Scenes

A Secret Worth Keeping 2

Ms. Nice Nasty

Ms. Nice Nasty: Cam's Confession

Sorority Ties

The Family That Lies

Dear God

And my Christian books: Doses of Devotion | You Only Live Once | Heroine Addict - Christian Women's Journal

Also available

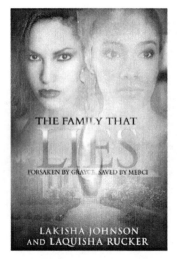

The Family that Lies

Born only months apart, Merci and Grayce Alexander were as close as sisters could get. With a father who thought the world of them, life was good. Until one day everything changed.

While Grayce got love and attention, Merci got all the hell, forcing her to leave home. She never looks back, putting the past behind her until … her sister shows up over a decade later begging for help, bringing all of the forgotten past with her. Merci wasn't the least bit prepared for what was about to happen next.

Merci realizes, she's been a part of something much bigger than she'd ever imagined. Yea, every family has their secrets, hidden truths and ties but Merci had no idea she'd been born into the family that lies.

https://www.amazon.com/Family-that-Lies-Lakisha-Johnson-ebook/dp/B01MAZD49X

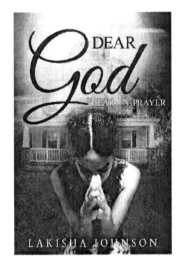

Dear God: Hear my Prayer

Since the age of 14, Jayme's life has been hell and she has one person to thank for it, Pastor James Madison.

He stood in the pulpit on Sundays waving the same hands that abused her at night. He glorified God with the same mouth he used to chip away her self-esteem, daily. He was a man of God who had turned her away from the same God he told people they needed to serve.

He was the man who was supposed to pray for, take care of and eventually love her. Instead he preyed on, took advantage of and shattered her heart before it had a chance to truly love someone else.

Now, 14 years and a son later, she finds herself needing God yet she doesn't know how to reach Him. She longs for God but isn't sure He can hear a sinner's prayer until she starts to say, Dear God.

https://www.amazon.com/Dear-God-Hear-My-Prayer-ebook/dp/B079G68BN3

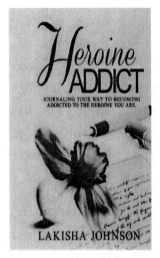

Christian Women's Journal – Heroine Addict

You are probably asking, why is this journal different from all the rest? After all, it is another book filled with blank pages intended for your thoughts, affirmations, poems, scriptures and etc.; however, this journal was created in the hope you will become addicted to heroine.

No, not the drug but the woman you are and destined to become. The woman who is admired by others, who is held in high regard, who is favorable and filled with courage. The woman who is honorable and of good quality. This journal was created, through prayer, in order to encourage you to search for, find, pull out and then display the heroine within you because your destiny depends on her surviving.

You can order through this link: https://www.paypal.me/AuthorLakisha/15

The Love that Lies between Us

By

Stacey Covington-Lee

Life is about relationships; they hurt and they heal. At times they are ugly, while others are incredibly beautiful, and what makes them so is the love. This collection of short stories explores the love that lies between man and woman, parent and child, lifelong friends, and ultimately, the love and respect we have for ourselves. Some of these stories are painful, others will make your heart soar. They are all laced with drama, romance, and are incredibly entertaining. As you get lost in the pages, you may find yourself reevaluating the love that lies between you and those that you allow in your life.

https://www.amazon.com/Love-That-Lies-Between-Us-ebook/dp/B078W37Y14

Her 13th Husband

By

B.M. Hardin

Ivy Raye had more than enough problems, but finding a husband wasn't one of them.

With 12 dead husbands in her past, she promised to make her 13th marriage last. Unfortunately, before she could get used to her new last name, fate started in on her, but this time; it played a different game.

In Ivy's world, things had always been the same: First comes Love. Then comes Pain. Yet, through lies, lust, murder and the unseen. She finds herself with a familiar problem: Who wants to kill Husband Thirteen?

https://www.amazon.com/Her-13th-Husband-B-M-Hardin-ebook/dp/B0784GNN47

CPSIA information can be obtained
at www.ICGtesting.com
Printed in the USA
LVOW10s1759020418
571970LV00011B/1092/P